THE DAILY CHARLES DICKENS

THE DAILY

CHARLES
DICKENS

A YEAR OF

QUOTES

Edited and with a Foreword by

JAMES R. KINCAID

The University of Chicago Press ✳ *Chicago and London*

The University of Chicago Press, Chicago 60637
The University of Chicago Press, Ltd., London
© 2018 by The University of Chicago
Published 2018
Printed in the United States of America

27 26 25 24 23 22 21 20 19 18   1 2 3 4 5

ISBN-13: 978-0-226-56374-9 (paper)
ISBN-13: 978-0-226-56388-6 (e-book)
DOI: https://doi.org/10.7208/chicago/9780226563886.001.0001

Library of Congress Cataloging-in-Publication Data

Names: Dickens, Charles, 1812–1870, author. | Kincaid, James R.
    (James Russell), editor, writer of foreword.
Title: The daily Charles Dickens : a year of quotes / Charles
    Dickens ; edited and with a foreword by James R. Kincaid.
Description: Chicago : The University of Chicago Press, 2018.
    | Includes index.
Identifiers: LCCN 2018014001 | ISBN 9780226563749 (pbk. : alk.
    paper) | ISBN 9780226563886 (e-book)
Subjects: LCSH: Dickens, Charles, 1812–1870—Quotations.
    | Quotations, English.
Classification: LCC PR4553 .K54 2018 | DDC 823/.8—dc23
LC record available at https://lccn.loc.gov/2018014001

Foreword

Of all the great writers, Dickens is the one most able to pack the highest voltage into the fewest words: to move us, amuse us, make us see what we had only dimly recognized before—and all in a flash.

This volume offers itself as an extended tribute to and illustration of that truth. Of course, it is not the only thing one might say about the source of Dickens's power and appeal. For some, testimonies to Dickens's epigrammatic talent, while true enough, pull them away from what they most love and admire about him: his cumulative force, the ways in which this supreme novelist of elaboration expands before us, building some of his finest effects through circling back on phrases, images, and scenes and developing them slowly.

We are, then, inside a most wondrous paradox: Dickens's power is produced both in sharp surprises and in slowly growing coils of accumulating energy.

I conducted a poll (very scientific) among Dickensian friends, asking them for their favorite quotes. About half responded with quick hitters—"Barkis is willin'" or "'Experientia does it!' as Papa used to say." The other half insisted that their favorite Dickens was not to be caged, that he was to be found at the top of his game in his most self-indulgent and brilliant moments, producing ever more lovely, moving, absurd instances of whatever occurs to him as he rolls along, economy of language be damned. I offer here a sample of this Dickens from *American Notes* (1842):

> About midnight we shipped a sea, which forced its way through the sky-lights, burst open the doors above, and came raging and roaring down into the ladies' cabin, to the unspeakable consternation of my wife and a little Scottish lady. . . . They and the handmaid . . . being in such ecstasies of fear that I scarcely knew what to do with them, I naturally bethought myself of some restorative or comfortable cordial; and nothing better occurring to me at the moment, than hot brandy-and-water, I procured a tumblerful without delay. It being impossible to stand or sit without holding on, they were all heaped together in one corner of a long sofa . . . where they clung to each other in momentary expectation of being drowned. When I approached this place with my specific, and was about to administer it with many consolatory expressions to the nearest sufferer, what was my dismay to see them all roll slowly down to the other end! And when I staggered to that end, and held out the glass once more, how immensely baffled were my good intentions by the ship giving another lurch, and their all rolling back again! I suppose I dodged them up and down this sofa for at least a quarter of an hour, without reaching them once; and by

the time I did catch them, the brandy-and-water was diminished by constant spilling to a teaspoon-ful.

This is the other, equally characteristic Dickens unleashing his open-ended play with language and its possibilities. Of course there is a kind of reporting going on here, but it's the reporting of someone who knows that storytelling has much to do with the minds and hearts of readers and little to do with "accuracy." Does anyone suppose Dickens really slid back and forth with the waves for a quarter of an hour? Was the brandy-and-water really dribbled down to a teaspoon? Who cares, right? His prose in instances such as this soars along on the wings of narrative richness, poetic fancy, and pure genius. He is never shackled by prosaic truth and thus so often reaches a higher and more penetrating truth.

Thus, we have mixed together in this volume full paragraphs (and more) with whammo phrases—and notable quotes from other writers and scholars. I have tried to go light on the very familiar quotes, those most readers will have access to in their own heads, and offered more from less popular locations and less well-known works. The problem has been deciding what not to include, how to leave on my yellow pads a couple hundred dazzlers I know you would love were I doing a "Two Years with Dickens" volume. But I suppose that makes no sense, alas.

I did, however, assume that our year with Dickens is a leap year. That way, we have 366 short and not-so-short daily visits with Dickens. Of course he is available always for longer invasions. You can even move in with him—with him and Oliver, David, Esther, Noddy Boffin, Amy Dorrit, and the Wellers. The welcome mat is always out.

THE DAILY CHARLES DICKENS

JANUARY

It was not a time for those who could by any means get light and warmth, to brave the fury of the weather. In coffee-houses of the better sort, guests crowded round the fire, forgot to be political, and told each other with a secret gladness that the blast grew fiercer every minute. Each humble tavern by the water-side, had its group of uncouth figures round the hearth, who talked of vessels foundering at sea, and all hands lost; related many a dismal tale of shipwreck and drowned men, and hoped that some they knew were safe, and shook their heads in doubt.

Barnaby Rudge (1841)

JANUARY 1

DOMBEY AND SON (1848)

There was a toothache in everything. The wine was so bitter cold that it forced a little scream from Miss Tox, which she had great difficulty in turning into a "Hem!" The veal had come from such an airy pantry, that the first taste of it had struck a sensation as of cold lead to Mr. Chick's extremities. Mr. Dombey alone remained unmoved. He might have been hung up for sale at a Russian fair as a specimen of a frozen gentleman.

JANUARY 2

MARTIN CHUZZLEWIT (1844)

"Ah!" said Bill [Simmons, coach driver] with a sigh . . . "Lummy Ned of the Light Salisbury, *he* was the one for musical talents. He *was* a guard. What you may call a Guard'an Angel, was Ned."

"Is he dead?" asked Martin.

"Dead!" replied the other, with a contemptuous emphasis. "Not he. You won't catch Ned a-dying easy. No, no. He knows better than that."

"For what are you, my young friend?" [asked Chadband.] "Are you a beast of the field? No. A bird of the air? No. A fish of the sea or river? No. You are a human boy, my young friend. A human boy. O glorious to be a human boy! And why glorious, my young friend? Because you are capable of receiving the lessons of wisdom, because you are capable of profiting by this discourse which I now deliver for your good, because you are not a stick, or a staff, or a stock, or a stone, or a post, or a pillar.

> O running stream of sparkling joy
> To be a soaring human boy!

And do you cool yourself in that stream now, my young friend? No. Why do you not cool yourself in that stream now? Because you are in a state of darkness, because you are in a state of obscurity . . . because you are in a state of bondage. My young friend, what is bondage? Let us, in a spirit of love, inquire."

"He is [said Elijah Pogrom] a true-born child of this free hemisphere! Verdant as the mountains of our country; bright and flowing as our mineral Licks; unspiled by withering conventionalities as air our broad and boundless Perearers! Rough he may be. So air our Barrs. Wild he may be. So air our Buffalers. But he is a child of Natur', and a child of Freedom; and his boastful answer to the Despot and the Tyrant is, that his bright home is in the Settin Sun."

"Stay, Satan, stay!" cried the preacher, as Kit was moving off.

"The gentleman says you're to stay, Christopher," whispered his mother.

"Stay, Satan, stay!" roared the preacher again. "Tempt not the woman that doth incline her ear to thee, but hearken to the voice of him that calleth. He hath a lamb from the fold!" cried the preacher, raising his voice still higher and pointing to the baby. "He beareth off a lamb, a precious lamb! . . ."

Kit was the best-tempered fellow in the world, but considering this strong language . . . [he] replied aloud:

"No, I don't. He's my brother."

"He's *my* brother!" cried the preacher.

"He isn't," said Kit indignantly. "How can you say such a thing? And don't call me names if you please; what harm have I done?"

JANUARY 6

"THE LAST CAB-DRIVER, AND THE FIRST OMNIBUS CAB," SKETCHES BY BOZ (1836)

We have studied the subject [getting out of a cab] a great deal, and we think the best way is, to throw yourself out, and trust to chance for alighting on your feet. If you make the driver alight first, and then throw yourself upon him, you will find that he breaks your fall materially.

JANUARY 7

"THE HAUNTED MAN," CHRISTMAS BOOKS (1848)

Everybody said so.

Far be it from me to assert that what everybody says must be true. Everybody is, often, as likely to be wrong as right. In the general experience, everybody has been wrong so often, and it has taken in most instances such a weary while to find out how wrong, that the authority is proved to be fallible. Everybody may sometimes be right; "but *that's* no rule," as the ghost of Giles Scroggins says in the ballad.

JANUARY 8
GREAT EXPECTATIONS (1861)

On our arrival in Denmark, we found the king and queen of that country elevated in two arm-chairs on a kitchen-table, holding a Court. The whole of the Danish nobility were in attendance; consisting of a noble boy in the wash-leather boots of a gigantic ancestor, a venerable Peer with a dirty face, who seemed to have risen from the people late in life, and the Danish chivalry with a comb in its hair and a pair of white silk legs, and presenting on the whole a feminine appearance. My gifted townsman stood gloomily apart, with folded arms, and I could have wished that his curls and forehead had been more probable.

JANUARY 9
THE MYSTERY OF EDWIN DROOD (1870)

Mr. Sapsea has many admirers. . . . He possesses the great qualities of being portentous and dull, and of having a roll in his speech, and another in his gait. . . . Voting at elections in the strictly respectable interest; morally satisfied that nothing but he himself has grown since he was a baby; how can dunderheaded Mr. Sapsea be otherwise than a credit to Cloisterham, and society?

JANUARY 10

"SCENES—CRIMINAL COURTS,"
SKETCHES BY BOZ (1836)

We shall never forget the mingled feelings of awe and respect with which we used to gaze on the exterior of Newgate in our schoolboy days. How dreadful its rough heavy walls, and low massive doors, appeared to us—the latter looking as if they were made for the express purpose of letting people in, and never letting them out again. Then the fetters over the debtors' door, which we used to think were a *bona fide* set of irons, just hung up there for convenience sake, ready to be taken down at a moment's notice, and riveted on the limbs of some refractory felon! We were never tired of wondering how the hackney-coachmen on the opposite stand could cut jokes in the presence of such horrors, and drink pots of half-and-half so near the last drop.

JANUARY 11

LETTER TO JOHN FORSTER (APRIL 13, 1856)

However strange it is to be never at rest, and never satisfied, and ever trying after something that is never reached, and to be always laden with plot and plan and care and worry, how clear it is that it must be. . . . It is much better to go and fret, than to stop and fret. As to repose—for some men there's no such thing in this life.

JANUARY 12

A TALE OF TWO CITIES (1859)

A tremendous roar arose from the throat of Saint Antoine, and a forest of naked arms struggled in the air like shrivelled branches of trees in a winter wind: all the fingers convulsively clutching at every weapon or semblance of a weapon that was thrown up from the depths below, no matter how far off.

. . . [M]uskets were being distributed—so were cartridges, powder, and ball, bars of iron and wood, knives, axes, pikes, every weapon that distracted ingenuity could discover or devise. . . . Every pulse and heart in Saint Antoine was on high-fever strain and at high-fever heat. Every living creature there held life as of no account, and was demented with a passionate readiness to sacrifice it.

JANUARY 13

"Do you live in London?" inquired Oliver.

"Yes. I do, when I'm at home," replied the boy. "I suppose you want some place to sleep in to-night, don't you?"

"I do, indeed," answered Oliver. "I have not slept under a roof since I left the country."

"Don't fret your eyelids on that score," said the young gentleman. "I've got to be in London to-night; and I know a 'spectable old genelman as lives there, wot'll give you lodgings for nothink, and never ask for the change—that is, if any genelman he knows interduces you. And don't he know me? Oh, no! Not in the least! By no means. Certainly not!"

JANUARY 14
A TALE OF TWO CITIES (1859)

Mr. Cruncher . . . always spoke of the year of our Lord as Anna Dominoes: apparently under the impression that the Christian era dated from the invention of a popular game, by a lady who had bestowed her name upon it.

JANUARY 15

OUR MUTUAL FRIEND (1865)

A grisly little fiction concerning her lovers is Lady Tippins's point. She is always attended by a lover or two, and she keeps a little list of her lovers, and she is always booking a new lover, or striking out an old lover, or putting a lover in her black list, or promoting a lover to her blue list, or adding up her lovers, or otherwise posting her book. Mrs. Veneering is charmed by the humour, and so is Veneering. Perhaps it is enhanced by a certain yellow play in Lady Tippins's throat, like the legs of scratching poultry.

JANUARY 16

THE OLD CURIOSITY SHOP (1841)

"I don't mean marrying [Nell] now"—returned the brother angrily; "say in two years' time, in three, in four. Does the old man look like a long-liver?"

"He don't look like it," said Dick, shaking his head, "but these old people—there's no trusting 'em, Fred. There's an aunt of mine down in Dorsetshire that was going to die when I was eight years old, and hasn't kept her word yet. They're so aggravating, so unprincipled, so spiteful—unless there's apoplexy in the family, Fred, you can't calculate upon 'em, and even then they deceive you just as often as not."

JANUARY 17
DAVID COPPERFIELD (1850)

"Again, I wonder with a sudden fear whether it is likely that our good old clergyman can be wrong, and Mr. and Miss Murdstone right, and that all the angels in Heaven can be destroying angels."

JANUARY 18
LITTLE DORRIT (1857)

There was old people, after working all their lives, going and being shut up in the workhouse, much worse fed and lodged and treated altogether, than— Mr. Plornish said manufacturers, but appeared to mean malefactors. Why, a man didn't know where to turn himself, for a crumb of comfort. As to who was to blame for it, Mr. Plornish didn't know who was to blame for it. He could tell you who suffered, but he couldn't tell you whose fault it was.

JANUARY 19
BLEAK HOUSE (1853)

When he has nothing else to do, he can always contemplate his own greatness. It is a considerable advantage to a man, to have so inexhaustible a subject.

There are books of which the backs and covers are by far the best parts.

Mr. Podsnap's notions of the Arts in their integrity might have been stated thus. Literature; large print, respectively descriptive of getting up at eight, shaving close at a quarter-past, breakfasting at nine, going to the City at ten, coming home at half-past five, and dining at seven. Painting and Sculpture; models and portraits representing Professors of getting up at eight, shaving close at a quarter-past, breakfasting at nine, going to the City at ten, coming home at half-past five, and dining at seven. Music; a respectable performance (without variations) on string and wind instruments, sedately expressive of getting up at eight, shaving close at a quarter-past, breakfasting at nine, going to the City at ten, coming home at half-past five, and dining at seven. Nothing else to be permitted to those same vagrants the Arts, on pain of excommunication. Nothing else To Be— anywhere!

Dombey sat in the corner of the darkened room in the great arm-chair by the bedside, and Son lay tucked up warm in a little basket bedstead, carefully disposed on a low settee immediately in front of the fire and close to it, as if his constitution were analogous to that of a muffin, and it was essential to toast him brown while he was very new.

Dombey was about eight-and-forty years of age. Son about eight-and-forty minutes. Dombey was rather bald, rather red, and though a handsome well-made man, too stern and pompous in appearance, to be prepossessing. Son was very bald, and very red, and though (of course) an undeniably fine infant, somewhat crushed and spotty in his general effect, as yet.

I don't feel any vulgar gratitude to you [for helping me]. I almost feel as if *you* ought to feel grateful to *me*, for giving you the opportunity of enjoying the luxury of generosity. . . . I may have been born to be a benefactor to you, by sometimes giving you an opportunity of assisting me.

MARK TWAIN ON ATTENDING A
DICKENS READING (AT STEINWAY HALL,
NEW YORK CITY) FEBRUARY 5, 1868

His pictures are hardly handsome, and he, like everybody else, is less handsome than his pictures. That fashion he has of brushing his hair and goatee so resolutely forward gives him a comical Scotch-terrier look about the face, which is rather heightened than otherwise by his portentous dignity and gravity. But that queer old head took on a sort of beauty, bye and bye, and a fascinating interest, as I thought of the wonderful mechanism within it, the complex but exquisitely adjusted machinery that could create men and women, and put the breath of life into them and alter all their ways and actions, elevate them, degrade them, murder them, marry them, conduct them through good and evil, through joy and sorrow, on their long march from the cradle to the grave, and never lose its godship over them, never make a mistake! I almost imagined I could see the wheels and pulleys work. This was Dickens—Dickens. There was no question about that, and yet it was not right easy to realize it. Somehow this puissant god seemed to be only a man, after all. How the great do tumble from their high pedestals when we see them in common human flesh, and know that they eat pork and cabbage and act like other men.

JANUARY 25

OLIVER TWIST (1838)

What an excellent example of the power of dress, young Oliver Twist was! Wrapped in the blanket which had hitherto formed his only covering, he might have been the child of a nobleman or a beggar; it would have been hard for the haughtiest stranger to have assigned him his proper station in society. But now that he was enveloped in the old calico robes which had grown yellow in the same service, he was badged and ticketed, and fell into his place at once—a parish child—the orphan of a workhouse— the humble, half-starved drudge—to be cuffed and buffeted through the world—despised by all, and pitied by none.

Oliver cried lustily. If he could have known that he was an orphan, left to the tender mercies of churchwardens and overseers, perhaps he would have cried the louder.

JANUARY 26

THE OLD CURIOSITY SHOP (1841)

"This poor little Marchioness has been wearing herself to death!" cried Dick.

"No I haven't," she returned, "not a bit of it. Don't you mind about me. I like sitting up, and I've often had a sleep, bless you, in one of them chairs. But if you could have seen how you tried to jump out o' winder, and if you could have heard how you used to keep on singing and making speeches, you wouldn't have believed it—I'm so glad you're better, Mr. Liverer."

"Liverer indeed!" said Dick thoughtfully. "It's well I *am* a liverer. I strongly suspect I should have died, Marchioness, but for you."

At this point, Mr. Swiveller took the small servant's hand in his, again, and being, as we have seen, but poorly, might in struggling to express his thanks have made his eyes as red as hers, but that she quickly changed the theme by making him lie down, and urging him to keep very quiet.

JANUARY 27
AMERICAN NOTES (1842)

We stopped to dine at Baltimore, and being now in Maryland, were waited on, for the first time, by slaves. The sensation of exacting any service from human creatures who are bought and sold, and being, for the time, a party as it were to their condition, is not an enviable one. The institution exists, perhaps, in its least repulsive and most mitigated form in such a town as this; but it *is* slavery; and though I was, with respect to it, an innocent man, its presence filled me with a sense of shame and self-reproach.

"Come on," said the jailer.

"Oh ah! I'll come on," replied the Dodger, brushing his hat with the palm of his hand. "Ah! (to the Bench) it's no use your looking frightened: I won't show you no mercy, not a ha'porth of it. *You'll* pay for this, my fine fellers. I wouldn't be you for something! I wouldn't go free, now, if you was to fall down on your knees and ask me. Here, carry me off to prison! Take me away!"

With these last words, the Dodger suffered himself to be led off by the collar; threatening, till he got into the yard, to make a parliamentary business of it; and then grinning in the officer's face, with great glee and self-approval.

The small teapot, and the single cup, had awakened in her mind sad recollections of Mr. Corney (who had not been dead more than five-and-twenty years); and she was overpowered.

"I shall never get another!" said Mrs. Corney, pettishly; "I shall never get another—like him."

Whether this remark bore reference to the husband, or the teapot, is uncertain. It might have been the latter; for Mrs. Corney looked at it as she spoke; and took it up afterwards.

JANUARY 30

"THE HAUNTED MAN," CHRISTMAS BOOKS (1848)

There might have been more pork on the knuckle-bone,—which knucklebone the carver at the cook's shop had assuredly not forgotten in carving for previous customers—but there was no stint of seasoning, and that is an accessory dreamily suggesting pork, and pleasantly cheating the sense of taste. The pease pudding, too, the gravy and mustard, . . . if they were not absolutely pork, had lived near it; so, upon the whole, there was the flavour of a middle-sized pig.

JANUARY 31

GREAT EXPECTATIONS (1861)

"Is [Miss Havisham] dead, Joe?"

"Why, you see, old chap," said Joe, in a tone of remonstrance, and by way of getting at it by degrees, "I wouldn't go so far as to say that, for that's a deal to say; but she ain't—"

"Living, Joe?"

"That's nigher where it is," said Joe; "she ain't living."

FEBRUARY

As it grew dusk, the wind fell; its distant moanings were more low and mournful; and, as it came creeping up the road, and rattling covertly among the dry brambles on either hand, it seemed like some great phantom for whom the way was narrow, whose garments rustled as it stalked along. By degrees it lulled and died away, and then it came on to snow.

The flakes fell fast and thick, soon covering the ground some inches deep, and spreading abroad a solemn stillness. The rolling wheels were noiseless, and the sharp ring and clatter of the horses' hoofs, became a dull, muffled tramp. The life of their progress seemed to be slowly hushed, and something death-like to usurp its place.

The Old Curiosity Shop (1841)

Bleak, dark, and piercing cold, it was a night for the well-housed and fed to draw round the bright fire and thank God they were at home; and for the homeless, starving wretch to lay him down and die. Many hunger-worn outcasts close their eyes in our bare streets, at such times, who, let their crimes have been what they may, can hardly open them in a more bitter world.

FEBRUARY 2

OUR MUTUAL FRIEND (1865)

"'Articulator of human bones'" [read Silas Wegg].

"That's it," with a groan. "That's it! Mr. Wegg. I'm thirty-two, and a bachelor. Mr. Wegg, I love her. Mr. Wegg, she is worthy of being loved by a Potentate!" Here Silas is rather alarmed by Mr. Venus springing to his feet in the hurry of his spirits, and haggardly confronting him with his hand on his coat collar; but Mr. Venus, begging pardon, sits down again, saying, with the calmness of despair, "She objects to the business."

"Does she know the profits of it?"

"She knows the profits of it, but she don't appreciate the art of it, and she objects to it. 'I do not wish,' she writes in her own handwriting, 'to regard myself, nor yet to be regarded, in that bony light.'"

FEBRUARY 3

Treachery don't come natural to beaming youth; but trust and pity, love and constancy,—they do, thank God!

FEBRUARY 4

"I have no learning, and you have much," said Milly; "I am not used to think, and you are always thinking. May I tell you why it seems to me a good thing for us to remember wrong that has been done us?"

"Yes."

"That we may forgive it."

FEBRUARY 5

And again he said "Dom-bey and Son," . . . .

Those three words conveyed the one idea of Mr. Dombey's life. The earth was made for Dombey and Son to trade in, and the sun and moon were made to give them light.

FEBRUARY 6

"Here's the gen'lm'n at last!" said one [coach-hire fellow], touching his hat with mock politeness. "Werry glad to see you, sir,—been a waitin' for you these six weeks. Jump in, if you please, sir!"

"Nice light fly and a fast trotter, sir," said another: "fourteen mile a hour, and surroundin' objects rendered inwisible by ex-treme welocity!"

"Large fly for your luggage, sir," cried a third. "Werry large fly here, sir—reg'lar bluebottle!"

"Here's *your* fly, sir!" shouted another aspiring charioteer, mounting the box, and inducing an old grey horse to indulge in some imperfect reminiscences of a canter. "Look at him, sir!—temper of a lamb and haction of a steam-ingein!"

FEBRUARY 7

To ladies and gentlemen who are not in the habit of devoting themselves practically to the science of penmanship, writing a letter is no very easy task; it being always considered necessary in such cases for the writer to recline his head on his left arm, so as to place his eyes as nearly as possible on a level with the paper, while glancing sideways at the letters he is constructing, to form with his tongue imaginary characters to correspond. These motions, although unquestionably of the greatest assistance to original composition, retard in some degree the progress of the writer.

FEBRUARY 8

"THE SHORT TIMERS,"
THE UNCOMMERCIAL TRAVELLER (1860)

[I]f the State would begin its work and duty at the beginning, and would with the strong hand take those children out of the streets, while they are yet children, and wisely train them, it would make them a part of England's glory, not its shame.

FEBRUARY 9

A TALE OF TWO CITIES (1859)

A terrible sound arose when the reading of this document [ordering a beheading] was done. A sound of craving and eagerness that had nothing articulate in it but blood. The narrative called up the most revengeful passions of the time, and there was not a head in the nation but must have dropped before it.

FEBRUARY 10

Mr. Grewgious . . . was an arid, sandy man, who, if he had been put into a grinding-mill, looked as if he would have ground immediately into high-dried snuff. He had a scanty flat crop of hair, in colour and consistency like some very mangy yellow fur tippet; it was so unlike hair, that it must have been a wig, but for the stupendous improbability of anybody's voluntarily sporting such a head.

FEBRUARY 11

"CHARACTERS—THOUGHTS ABOUT PEOPLE," SKETCHES BY BOZ (1836)

It is strange with how little notice, good, bad, or indifferent, a man may live and die in London. He awakens no sympathy in the breast of any single person; his existence is a matter of interest to no one save himself; he cannot be said to be forgotten when he dies, for no one remembered him when he was alive.

FEBRUARY 12

LETTER TO JOHN FORSTER (FEBRUARY 3, 1855)

Why is it, that as with poor David, a sense comes always crushing on me now, when I fall into low spirits, as of one happiness I have missed in life, one friend and companion I have never made?

FEBRUARY 13

THE OLD CURIOSITY SHOP (1841)

"Before I'd let a man order me about as Quilp orders her," said Mrs. George; "before I'd consent to stand in awe of a man as she does of him, I'd—I'd kill myself, and write a letter first to say he did it!"

FEBRUARY 14

THE PICKWICK PAPERS (1837)

"'So I take the privilidge of the day, Mary, my dear—as the gen'l'm'n in difficulties did, ven he valked out of a Sunday,—to tell you that the first and only time I see you, your likeness was took on my hart in much quicker time and brighter colours than ever a likeness was took by the profeel macheen (wich p'raps you may have heerd on Mary my dear) altho it *does* finish a portrait and put the frame and glass on complete, with a hook at the end to hang it up by, and all in two minutes and a quarter.'"

"I am afeerd that werges on the poetical, Sammy," said Mr. Weller, dubiously.

"No it don't," replied Sam, reading on very quickly, to avoid contesting the point:

"'Except of me Mary my dear as your walentine and think over what I've said.—My dear Mary I will now conclude.' That's all," said Sam.

"That's rather a sudden pull up, ain't it, Sammy?" inquired Mr. Weller.

"Not a bit on it," said Sam; "she'll vish there wos more, and that's the great art o' letter writin.'"

FEBRUARY 15

DAVID COPPERFIELD (1850)

"It may be" [David said,] "profitable to you to reflect, in future, that there never were greed and cunning in the world yet, that did not do too much, and over-reach themselves. It is as certain as death."

"Or as certain as they used to teach at school (the same school where I picked up so much umbleness), from nine o'clock to eleven, that labour was a curse; and from eleven o'clock to one, that it was a blessing and a cheerfulness, and a dignity, and I don't know what all, eh?" said [Uriah] with a sneer. "You preach, about as consistent as they did."

"He's going to die here, after all. Going to die upon the premises. Going to die in our house!"

"And where should he have died, Tugby?" cried his wife.

"In the workhouse," he returned. "What are workhouses made for?"

"You might, from your appearance, be the wife of Lucifer," said Miss Pross in her breathing. "Nevertheless, you shall not get the better of me. I am an Englishwoman."

The smallest boy I ever conversed with, carrying the largest baby I ever saw, offered a supernaturally intelligent explanation of [the Marshalsea Prison area] in its old uses. . . . How this young Newton (for such I judge him to be) came by his information, I don't know; he was a quarter of a century too young to know anything about it of himself. I pointed to the window of the room where Little Dorrit was born . . . and asked him what was the name of the lodger who tenanted that apartment at present? He said, "Tom Pythick." I asked him who was Tom Pythick? and he said, "Joe Pythick's uncle."

FEBRUARY 19

"THE STREETS—MORNING, 'SCENES,'" SKETCHES BY BOZ (1836)

The last drunken man, who shall find his way home before sunlight, has just staggered heavily along, roaring out the burden of the drinking song of the previous night: the last homeless vagrant whom penury and police have left in the streets, has coiled up his chilly limbs in some paved corner, to dream of food and warmth. The drunken, the dissipated, and the wretched have disappeared; the more sober and orderly part of the population have not yet awakened to the labours of the day, and the stillness of death is over the streets; its very hue seems to be imparted to them, cold and lifeless as they look in the grey, sombre light of daybreak.

FEBRUARY 20

"Here's this morning's New York Sewer!" cried one. "Here's this morning's New York Stabber! Here's the New York Family Spy! Here's the New York Private Listener! Here's the New York Peeper! Here's the New York Plunderer! Here's the New York Keyhole Reporter! Here's the New York Rowdy Journal! Here's all the New York papers! Here's full particulars of the patriotic loco-foco movement yesterday, in which the whigs was so chawed up; and the last Alabama gouging case; and the interesting Arkansas dooel with Bowie knives."

FEBRUARY 21

OUR MUTUAL FRIEND (1865)

A certain institution in Mr. Podsnap's mind which he called "the young person" may be considered to have been embodied in Miss Podsnap, his daughter. It was an inconvenient and exacting institution, as requiring everything in the universe to be filed down and fitted to it. The question about everything was, would it bring a blush into the cheek of the young person? And the inconvenience of the young person was that, according to Mr. Podsnap, she seemed always liable to burst into blushes when there was no need at all. There appeared to be no line of de-

marcation between the young person's excessive in-
nocence, and another person's guiltiest knowledge.

FEBRUARY 22

There was a man on board this boat . . . who was the
most inquisitive fellow that can possibly be imagined. He never spoke otherwise than interrogatively.
He was an embodied inquiry. . . . Every button in his
clothes said, "Eh? What's that? Did you speak? Say
that again, will you?" . . . .

I wore a fur great-coat at that time, and before
we were well clear of the wharf, he questioned me
concerning it, and its price, and where I bought it,
and when, and what fur it was, and what it weighed,
and what it cost. Then he took notice of my watch,
and asked me what *that* cost, and whether it was
a French watch, and where I had got it, and how I
got it, whether I bought it or had it given me, and
how it went, and where the key-hole was, and when
I wound it, every night or every morning, and whether I ever forgot to wind it at all, and if I did, what
then? Where had I been to last, and where was I going next, and where was I going after that, and had
I seen the President, and what did he say, and what
did I say, and what did he say when I had said that?
Eh? Lor now! do tell!

FEBRUARY 23
OLIVER TWIST (1838)

The gruel disappeared; the boys whispered each other, and winked at Oliver; while his next neighbours nudged him. Child as he was, he was desperate with hunger, and reckless with misery. He rose from the table; and advancing to the master, basin and spoon in hand, said: somewhat alarmed at his own temerity:

"Please, sir, I want some more."

The master was a fat, healthy man; but he turned very pale. He gazed in stupefied astonishment on the small rebel for some seconds, and then clung for support to the copper. The assistants were paralysed with wonder; the boys with fear.

"What!" said the master at length, in a faint voice.

"Please, sir," replied Oliver, "I want some more."

FEBRUARY 24
BARNABY RUDGE (1841)

.... Mr. Willet arose from table, walked round to Joe, felt his empty sleeve all the way up, from the cuff, to where the stump of his arm remained; shook his hand; lighted his pipe at the fire, took a long whiff, walked to the door, turned round once when he had reached it, wiped his left eye with the back of his forefinger, and said, in a faltering voice; "My

son's arm—was took off—at the defense of the—
Salwanners—in America—where the war is"—with
which words he withdrew, and returned no more
that night.

FEBRUARY 25
GREAT EXPECTATIONS (1861)

"Pip, dear old chap, life is made of ever so many
partings welded together. . . . Diwisions among such
must come, and must be met as they come. If there's
been any fault at all to-day, it's mine. . . . I'm wrong
out of the forge, the kitchen, or off th' meshes. You
won't find half so much fault in me if you think of
me in my forge dress, with my hammer in my hand,
or even my pipe. You won't find half so much fault
in me if, supposing as you should ever wish to see
me, you come and put your head in at the forge window and see Joe the blacksmith, there, at the old
anvil. . . . And so God bless you, dear old Pip, old
chap, God bless you!"

FEBRUARY 26
OUR MUTUAL FRIEND (1865)

"About how long might it take you now, at a average
rate of going, to be a Judge?" asked Mr. Boffin [of the
clerk], after surveying his small stature in silence.

The boy answered that he had not quite worked out that little calculation.

"I suppose there's nothing to prevent you going in for it?" said Mr. Boffin.

The boy virtually replied that as he had the honour to be a Briton who never, never, never, there was nothing to prevent his going in for it. Yet he seemed inclined to suspect that there might be something to prevent his coming out with it.

FEBRUARY 27

THE OLD CURIOSITY SHOP (1841)

"It's a devil of a thing, gentlemen," said Mr. Swiveller, "when relations fall out and disagree. If the wing of friendship should never moult a feather, the wing of relationship should never be clipped, but be always expanded and serene. Why should a grandson and grandfather peg away at each other with mutual wiolence when all might be bliss and concord? Why not jine hands and forget it?"

FEBRUARY 28

VILLAGER'S SONG, FROM "THE CHIMES,"

CHRISTMAS BOOKS (1844)

"O let us love our occupations,
Bless the squire and his relations,
Live upon our daily rations,
And always know our proper stations."

FEBRUARY 29

GREAT EXPECTATIONS (1861)

With an alphabet on the hearth at my feet for reference, I contrived in an hour or two to print and smear this epistle:

MI DEER JO i OPE U r KRWITE WELL i OPE i
SHAL SON B HABELL 4 2 TEEDGE U JO AN THEN
WE SHORL B SO GLODD AN WEN i M PRENGTD 2
U JO WOT LARX AN BLEVE ME INF XN PIP.

MARCH

It was one of those March days when the sun shines hot and the wind blows cold: when it is summer in the light, and winter in the shade.

Great Expectations (1861)

MARCH 1

NICHOLAS NICKLEBY (1839)

Love, however, is very materially assisted by a warm and active imagination: which has a long memory, and will thrive for a considerable time on very slight and sparing food.

MARCH 2

DAVID COPPERFIELD (1850)

"My other piece of advice, Copperfield," said Mr. Micawber, "you know. Annual income twenty pounds, annual expenditure nineteen nineteen six, result happiness. Annual income twenty pounds, annual expenditure twenty pounds ought and six, result misery. The blossom is blighted, the leaf is withered, the God of day goes down upon the dreary scene, and—and in short you are for ever floored. As I am!"

MARCH 3

THE PICKWICK PAPERS (1837)

[On the occasion of Mr. Tupman donning a green velvet jacket and Mr. Pickwick questioning if he means actually to wear it.]

"Such *is* my intention, sir," replied Mr. Tupman warmly. "And why not, sir?"

"Because, sir," said Mr. Pickwick, considerably excited, "Because you are too old, sir."

"Too old!" exclaimed Mr. Tupman.

"And if any further ground of objection be wanting," continued Mr. Pickwick, "you are too fat, sir."

"Sir," said Mr. Tupman, his face suffused with a crimson glow. "This is an insult."

"Sir," replied Mr. Pickwick, in the same tone, "It is not half the insult to you, that your appearance in my presence in a green velvet jacket, with a two-inch tail, would be to me."

MARCH 4

THE OLD CURIOSITY SHOP (1841)

"Don't you feel how naughty it is of you," resumed Miss Monflathers [to Nell], "to be a wax-work child, when you might have the proud consciousness of assisting, to the extent of your infant powers, the manufactures of your country; of improving your mind by the constant contemplation of the steam-engine; and of earning a comfortable and independent subsistence of from two-and-ninepence to three shillings per week? Don't you know that the harder you are at work, the happier you are?"

Conceive the situation of a man, spending his last night on earth in this cell. Buoyed up with some vague and undefined hope of reprieve, he knew not why—indulging in some wild and visionary idea of escaping, he knew not how—hour after hour of the three preceding days allowed him for preparation, has fled with a speed which no man living would deem possible, for none but this dying man can know.

Through this vast throng, sprinkled doubtless here and there with honest zealots, but composed for the most part of the very scum and refuse of London, whose growth was fostered by bad criminal laws, bad prison regulations, and the worst conceivable police, such of the members of both Houses of Parliament as had not taken the precaution to be already at their posts, were compelled to fight and force their way. Their carriages were stopped and broken; the wheels wrenched off; the glasses shivered to atoms; the panels beaten in; drivers, footmen, and masters, pulled from their seats and rolled in the mud.

MARCH 7

"There are some happy creeturs," Mrs. Gamp observed, "as time runs back'ards with, and you are one Mrs. Mould; not that he need do nothing except use you in his most owldacious way for years to come, I'm sure; for young you are and will be."

MARCH 8

To appeal to [Madame Defarge], was made hopeless by her having no sense of pity, even for herself. If she had been laid low in the streets . . . she would not have pitied herself; nor, if she had been ordered to the axe to-morrow, would she have gone to it with any softer feeling than a fierce desire to change places with the man who sent her there.

MARCH 9

"And" [said Joe], "last of all, Pip—and this I want to say very serious to you, old chap—I see so much in my poor mother, of a woman drudging and slaving and breaking her honest hart and never getting no peace in her mortal days, that I'm dead afeerd of going wrong in the way of not doing what's right by a woman, and I'd fur rather of the two go wrong the t'other way, and be a little ill-conwenienced myself. I wish it were only me put out, Pip . . . , and I hope you'll overlook shortcomings."

Young as I was, I believe that I dated a new admiration of Joe from that night. We were equals afterwards, as we had been before; but, afterwards at quiet times when I sat looking at Joe and thinking about him, I had a new sensation of feeling conscious that I was looking up to Joe in my heart.

MARCH 10

AMERICAN NOTES (1842)

Pittsburg [sic] is like Birmingham in England; at least its townspeople say so. Setting aside the streets, the shops, the houses, waggons, factories, public buildings, and population, perhaps it may be.

MARCH 11

DAVID COPPERFIELD (1850)

"Procrastination is the thief of time. Collar him!"

MARCH 12

It is a dreadful thing to wait and watch for the approach of death; to know that hope is gone, and recovery impossible; and to sit and count the dreary hours through long, long nights—such nights as only watchers by the bed of sickness know. It chills the blood to hear the dearest secrets of the heart . . . poured forth by the unconscious helpless being before you; and to think how little the reserve and cunning of a whole life will avail, when fever and delirium tear off the mask at last.

MARCH 13

MARTIN CHUZZLEWIT (1844)

"Moralise as we will, the world goes on [said Mr. Tigg]. As Hamlet says, Hercules may lay about him with his club in every possible direction, but he can't prevent the cats from making a most intolerable row on the roofs of the houses, or the dogs from being shot in the hot weather if they run about the streets unmuzzled. Life's a riddle: a most infernally hard riddle to guess, Mr. Pecksniff. My own opinion is, that like the celebrated conundrum, 'Why's a man in jail like a man out of jail?' there's no answer to it. Upon my soul and body, it's the queerest sort of thing altogether—but there's no use in talking about it. Ha! ha!"

MARCH 14

BLEAK HOUSE (1853)

"Your mother, Esther, is your disgrace, and you were hers. The time will come—and soon enough—when you will understand this better, and will feel it too, as no one save a woman can."

MARCH 15

THE PICKWICK PAPERS (1837)

"Heads, heads—take care of your heads!" cried the loquacious stranger, as they came out under the low archway, which in those days formed the entrance to the coach-yard. "Terrible place—dangerous work —other day—five children—mother—tall lady, eating sandwiches—forgot the arch—crash—knock—children look round—mother's head off—sandwich in her hand—no mouth to put it in—head of a family off—shocking, shocking!"

THE OLD CURIOSITY SHOP (1841)

"How's the Giant?" said Short, when they all sat smoking round the fire.

"Rather weak upon his legs," returned Mr. Vuffin. "I begin to be afraid he's going at the knees."

"That's a bad look-out," said Short.

"Aye! Bad indeed," replied Mr. Vuffin, contemplating the fire with a sigh. "Once get a giant shaky on his legs, and the public care no more about him than they do for a dead cabbage-stalk."

MARCH 17

BLEAK HOUSE (1853)

Jo lives—that is to say, Jo has not yet died—in a ruinous place, known to the like of him by the name of Tom-all-Alone's. It's a black, dilapidated street, avoided by all decent people: where the crazy houses were seized upon, when their decay was far advanced, by some bold vagrants, who, after establishing their own possession, took to letting them out in lodgings. Now, these tumbling tenements contain, by night, a swarm of misery.

"Guard! What place is this?"

"Mugby Junction, Sir."

"A windy place!"

"Yes, it mostly is, Sir."

"And looks comfortless indeed!"

"Yes, it generally does, Sir."

"Is it a rainy night still?"

"Pours, Sir."

"Open the door. I'll get out."

MARCH 19

BARNABY RUDGE (1841)

"Oh, Johnny," said Solomon, shaking him by the hand. "Oh, Parkes. Oh, Tommy Cobb. Why did I leave this house to-night! On the nineteenth of March—of all nights in the year, on the nineteenth of March!"

They all drew closer to the fire. Parkes, who was nearest to the door, started and looked over his shoulder. Mr. Willet, with great indignation, inquired what the devil he meant by that—and then said, "God forgive me," and glanced over his own shoulder, and came a little nearer.

MARCH 20

"Dombey, come along!" cried the Major, looking in at the door. "Damme, Sir, old Joe has a great mind to propose an alteration in the name of the Royal Hotel, and that it should be called the Three Jolly Bachelors, in honour of ourselves and Carker." With this, the Major slapped Mr. Dombey on the back, and winking over his shoulder at the ladies, with a frightful tendency of blood to the head, carried him off.

MARCH 21

Miss La Creevy [the miniature painter] had got up early to put a fancy nose into a miniature of an ugly little boy, destined for his grandmother in the country, who was expected to bequeath him property if he was like the family.

"To carry out an idea," repeated Miss La Creevy; "and that's the great convenience of living in a thoroughfare like the Strand. When I want a nose or an eye for any particular sitter, I have only to look out of window and wait till I get one."

MARCH 22

HARD TIMES (1854)

"I was born [said Bounderby] in a ditch, and my mother ran away from me. Do I excuse her for it? No. Have I ever excused her for it? Not I. What do I call her for it? I call her probably the very worst woman that ever lived in the world, except my drunken grandmother. There's no family pride about me, there's no imaginative sentimental humbug about me."

MARCH 23

LITTLE DORRIT (1857)

"And good-bye, John," said Little Dorrit. "And I hope you will have a good wife one day, and be a happy man. I am sure you will deserve to be happy, and you will be, John."

As she held out her hand to him with these words, the heart that was under the waistcoat of sprigs—mere slop-work, if the truth must be known—swelled to the size of the heart of a gentleman; and the poor common little fellow, having no room to hold it, burst into tears.

MARCH 24

"THE HOSPITAL PATIENT—CHARACTERS,"
SKETCHES BY BOZ (1836)

About a twelvemonth ago, as we were strolling through Covent Garden . . . we were attracted by the very prepossessing appearance of a pickpocket, who having declined to take the trouble of walking to the Police Office, on the ground that he hadn't the slightest wish to go there at all, was being conveyed thither in a wheelbarrow, to the huge delight of a crowd.

MARCH 25

BARNABY RUDGE (1841)

It was, in fact, the twenty-fifth of March, which, as most people know to their cost, is, and has been time out of mind, one of those unpleasant epochs termed quarter-days.

MARCH 26

"Now you two gentlemen have business to discuss, I know," said the doctor, "and your time is precious. So is mine; for several lives are waiting for me in the next room, and I have a round of visits to make after—after I have taken 'em."

MARCH 27

"CHARACTERS—THE PARLOUR ORATOR,"
SKETCHES BY BOZ (1836)

"What is a man?" continued the red-faced [man], jerking his hat indignantly from its peg on the wall. "What is an Englishman? Is he to be trampled upon by every oppressor? Is he to be knocked down at everybody's bidding? What's freedom? Not a standing army. What's a standing army? Not freedom. What's general happiness? Not universal misery. Liberty ain't the window-tax, is it? The Lords ain't the Commons, are they?" And the red-faced man, gradually bursting into a radiating sentence, in which such adjectives as "dastardly," "oppressive," "violent," and "sanguinary," formed the most conspicuous words, knocked his hat indignantly over his eyes, left the room, and slammed the door after him.

"Wonderful man!" said he of the sharp nose.

"Splendid speaker!" added the broker.

We went to the ragged bundle nearest to the Workhouse-door, and I touched it. No movement replying, I gently shook it. The rags began to be slowly stirred within, and by little and little a head was unshrouded. The head of a woman of three or four and twenty, as I should judge; gaunt with want, and foul with dirt; but not naturally ugly.

"Tell us," said I, stooping down. "Why are you lying here?"

"Because I can't get into the Workhouse." She spoke in a faint dull way, and had no curiosity or interest left. She looked drearily at the black sky and the falling rain, but never looked at me or my companion.

"Were you here last night?"

"Yes. All last night. And the night afore too."

MARCH 29

"THE BROKER'S MAN—OUR PARISH,"
SKETCHES BY BOZ (1836)

[Mr. Bung] is not, as he forcibly remarks, "one of those fortunate men who, if they were to dive under one side of a barge stark-naked, would come up on the other with a new suit of clothes on, and a ticket or soup in the waistcoat-pocket:" neither is he one of those whose spirit has been broken beyond redemption by misfortune and want. He is just one of the careless, good-for-nothing, happy fellows, who float, cork-like, on the surface, for the world to play at hockey with.

MARCH 30

DAVID COPPERFIELD (1850)

"I will never desert Mr. Micawber. Mr. Micawber may have concealed his difficulties from me in the first instance, but his sanguine temper may have led him to expect that he would overcome them. The pearl necklace and bracelets which I inherited from mama, have been disposed of for less than half their value; and the set of coral, which was the wedding gift of my papa, has been actually thrown away for nothing. But I will never desert Mr. Micawber. No!" cried Mrs. Micawber, more affected than before, "I never will do it! It's of no use asking me!"

MARCH 31

THE OLD CURIOSITY SHOP (1841)

"But what," said Mr. Swiveller with a sigh, "what is the odds so long as the fire of soul is kindled at the taper of conwiviality, and the wing of friendship never moults a feather! What is the odds so long as the spirit is expanded by means of rosy wine, and the present moment is the least happiest of our existence!"

APRIL

It was on one of those mornings, common in early spring, when the year, fickle and changeable in its youth like all other created things, is undecided whether to step backward into winter or forward into summer, and in its uncertainty inclines now to one and now to the other, and now to both at once— wooing summer in the sunshine, and lingering still with winter in the shade—it was, in short . . . one of those mornings when it is hot and cold, wet and dry, bright and lowering, sad and cheerful, withering and genial, in the compass of one short hour.

Barnaby Rudge (1841)

Sir,

I was raised in those interminable solitudes where our mighty Mississippi (or Father of Waters) rolls his turbid flood.

I am young, and ardent. For there is a poetry in wildness, and every alligator basking in the slime is in himself an Epic, self-contained. I aspirate for fame. It is my yearning and my thirst.

Are you, sir, aware of any member of Congress in England, who would undertake to pay my expenses to that country, and for six months after my arrival?

There is something within me which gives me the assurance that this enlightened patronage would not be thrown away. In literature or art; the bar, the pulpit, or the stage; in one or other, if not all, I feel that I am certain to succeed.

If too much engaged to write to any such yourself, please let me have a list of three or four of those most likely to respond, and I will address them through the Post Office. May I also ask you to favour me with any critical observations that have ever presented themselves to your reflective faculties, on "Cain: a Mystery," by the Right Honourable Lord Byron?

I am, Sir,
Yours (forgive me if I add, soaringly),
Putnam Smif.

APRIL 2

OUR MUTUAL FRIEND (1865)

As some dogs have it in the blood, or are trained, to worry certain creatures to a certain point, so—not to make the comparison disrespectfully—Pleasant Riderhood had it in the blood, or had been trained, to regard seamen, within certain limits, as her prey. Show her a man in a blue jacket, and, figuratively speaking, she pinned him instantly.

APRIL 3

BARNABY RUDGE (1841)

"What *have* I done?" reasoned poor Joe.

"Silence, sir!" returned [old Willet], "what do you mean by talking, when you see people that are more than two or three times your age, sitting still and silent and not dreaming of saying a word?"

"Why that's the proper time for me to talk, isn't it?" said Joe rebelliously.

"The proper time, sir!" retorted his father, "the proper time's no time."

APRIL 4

"Take another glass of wine, and excuse my mentioning that society as a body does not expect one to be so strictly conscientious in emptying one's glass, as to turn it bottom upwards with the rim on one's nose."

APRIL 5

"Well, it's no use talking about it now," said Sam. "It's over, and can't be helped, and that's one consolation, as they always says in Turkey, ven they cuts the wrong man's head off."

APRIL 6

"Mine ain't a selfish affection, you know," said Mr. Toots, in the confidence engendered by his having been a witness of the Captain's tenderness. "It's the sort of thing with me, Captain Gills, that if I could be run over—or—or trampled upon—or—or thrown off a very high place—or anything of that sort—for Miss Dombey's sake, it would be the most delightful thing that could happen to me."

"I am an old woman now and my good looks are gone but that's me my dear over the plate-warmer and considered like in the times when you used to pay two guineas on ivory and took your chance pretty much how you came out, which made you very careful how you left it about afterwards because people were turned so red and uncomfortable by mostly guessing it was somebody else quite different, and there was once a certain person that had put his money in a hop business that came in one morning to pay his rent and his respects being the second floor that would have taken it down from the hook and put it in his breast-pocket. . . . [A]nd I think myself it *was* like me when I was young and wore that sort of stays."

"I don't wish to make a display of my feelings, but I have habitually thought of you more in the night than I am quite equal to."

"Then don't think of me," retorted Miss Havisham.

"Very easily said!" remarked Camilla, amiably

repressing a sob, while a hitch came into her upper lip, and her tears overflowed. "Raymond is a witness what ginger and sal volatile I am obliged to take in the night. Raymond is a witness what nervous jerkings I have in my legs. Chokings and nervous jerkings, however, are nothing new to me when I think with anxiety of those I love."

APRIL 9

OLIVER TWIST (1838)

"[Chimney-sweeping's] a nasty trade," said Mr. Limbkins. . . .

"Young boys have been smothered in chimneys before now," said another gentleman.

"That's acause they damped the straw afore they lit it in the chimbley to make 'em come down agin," said Gamfield; "that's all smoke, and no blaze; verass smoke ain't o' no use at all in making a boy come down, for it only sinds him to sleep, and that's wot he likes. Boys is wery obstinit, and wery lazy, gen'lmen, and there's nothink like a good hot blaze to make 'em come down vith a run. It's humane too, gen'lmen, acause, even if they've stuck in the chimbley, roasting their feet makes 'em struggle to hextricate theirselves."

APRIL 10
HARD TIMES (1854)

[Coketown] was a town of red brick, or of brick that would have been red if the smoke and ashes had allowed it; but as matters stood it was a town of unnatural red and black like the painted face of a savage. It was a town of machinery and tall chimneys, out of which interminable serpents of smoke trailed themselves for ever and ever, and never got uncoiled.

APRIL 11
LITTLE DORRIT (1857)

"Rattle me out of bed early, set me going, give me as short a time as you like to bolt my meals in, and keep me at it. Keep me always at it, and I'll keep you always at it, you keep somebody else always at it. There you are with the Whole Duty of Man in a commercial country."

APRIL 12
THE OLD CURIOSITY SHOP (1841)

"I can almost fancy," said the lawyer [Sampson Brass], shaking his head, "that I see his eye glistening down at the very bottom of my liquor. When shall we look upon [Quilp's] like again? Never, never! One minute we are here"—holding his tumbler before his eyes—"the next we are there"—gulping down its contents, and striking himself emphatically a little below the chest—"in the silent tomb. To think I should be drinking his very rum! It seems like a dream."

APRIL 13
NICHOLAS NICKLEBY (1839)

"Why, then, I'll tell you [an occupation]," said Mr. Crummles, throwing his pipe into the fire, and raising his voice. "The stage."

"The stage!" cried Nicholas in a voice almost as loud.

"The theatrical profession," said Mr. Vincent Crummles. "I am in the theatrical profession myself, my wife is in the theatrical profession, my children are in the theatrical profession. I had a dog that lived and died in it from a puppy; and my chaise-pony goes on, in Timour the Tartar. I'll bring you out, and your friend too. Say the word. I want a novelty."

"I don't know anything about it," rejoined Nicholas, whose breath had been almost taken away from him by this sudden proposal. "I never acted a part in my life, except at school."

"There's genteel comedy in your walk and manner, juvenile tragedy in your eye, and touch-and-go farce in your laugh," said Mr. Vincent Crummles. "You'll do as well as if you had thought of nothing else but the lamps, from your birth downwards."

APRIL 14

LETTER TO GEORGE DOLBY (SEPTEMBER 25, 1868)

I can't get my hat on in consequence of the extent to which my hair stands on end at the costs and charges of these boys. Why was I ever a father!

APRIL 15

LITTLE DORRIT (1857)

Mr. Merdle took down a countess who was secluded somewhere in the core of an immense dress, to which she was in the proportion of the heart to the overgrown cabbage.

APRIL 16

DAVID COPPERFIELD (1850)

"Oh, my eyes and limbs!" [the dealer in secondhand clothes] then cried, peeping hideously out of the shop, after a long pause, "will you go for twopence more?"

"I can't," I said; "I shall be starved."

"Oh, my lungs and liver, will you go for three-pence?"

"I would go for nothing, if I could," I said, "but I want the money badly."

"Oh go—roo!" (it is really impossible to express how he twisted this ejaculation out of himself, as he peeped round the doorpost at me, showing nothing but his crafty old head;) "will you go for fourpence?"

APRIL 17

MASTER HUMPHREY'S CLOCK (1840–41)

To conceal anything from those to whom I am attached, is not in my nature. I can never close my lips where I have opened my heart.

APRIL 18

GREAT EXPECTATIONS (1861)

So, I came into Smithfield; and the shameful place, being all asmear with filth and fat and blood and foam, seemed to stick to me. So I rubbed it off with all possible speed by turning into a street where I saw the great black dome of Saint Paul's bulging at me from behind a grim stone building which a by-stander said was Newgate Prison.

APRIL 19

LITTLE DORRIT (1857)

The Circumlocution Office was (as everybody knows without being told) the most important Department under Government. No public business of any kind could possibly be done at any time, without the acquiescence of the Circumlocution Office. Its finger was in the largest public pie, and in the smallest public tart. . . . If another Gunpowder Plot had been discovered half an hour before the lighting of the match, nobody would have been justified in saving the parliament until there had been half a score of boards, half a bushel of minutes, several sacks of official memoranda, and a family-vault full of ungrammatical correspondence, on the part of the Circumlocution Office.

APRIL 20

AMERICAN NOTES (1842)

When we [Dickens and a Choctaw native] shook hands at parting, I told him he must come to England . . . that . . . he would be well received and kindly treated. He was evidently pleased by this assurance, though he rejoined with a good-humoured smile and an arch shake of his head, that the English used to be very fond of the Red Men when they wanted their help, but had not cared much for them, since.

APRIL 21

"THE BLOOMSBURY CHRISTENING—TALES,"
SKETCHES BY BOZ (1836)

Mr. Nicodemus Dumps, or, as his acquaintance called him, "long Dumps," was a bachelor, six feet high, and fifty years old: cross, cadaverous, odd, and ill-natured. He was never happy but when he was miserable; and always miserable when he had the best reason to be happy. . . . He was familiar with the face of every tombstone, and the burial service seemed to excite his strongest sympathy. His friends said he was surly—he insisted he was nervous; they thought him a lucky dog, but he protested that he was "the most unfortunate man in the world."

APRIL 22

THE OLD CURIOSITY SHOP (1841)

In this depressed state of the classical market, Mrs. Jarley made extraordinary efforts to stimulate the popular taste, and whet the popular curiosity. Certain machinery in the body of the nun on the leads over the door was cleaned up and put in motion, so that the figure shook its head paralytically all day long, to the great admiration of a drunken, but very Protestant, barber over the way, who looked upon the said paralytic motion as typical of the degrading effect wrought upon the human mind by the ceremonies of the Romish Church, and discoursed upon that theme with great eloquence and morality. . . . Mrs. Jarley sat in the pay-place, chinking silver moneys from noon till night, and solemnly calling upon the crowd to take notice that the price of admission was only sixpence, and that the departure of the whole collection, on a short tour among the Crowned Heads of Europe, was positively fixed for that day week.

APRIL 23

DOMBEY AND SON (1848)

They were assembled in Cleopatra's room. The Serpent of old Nile (not to mention her disrespectfully) was reposing on her sofa, sipping her morning chocolate at three o'clock in the afternoon, and Flowers the Maid was fastening on her youthful cuffs and frills, and performing a kind of private coronation ceremony on her, with a peach-coloured velvet bonnet; the artificial roses in which nodded to uncommon advantage, as the palsy trifled with them, like a breeze.

APRIL 24
OLIVER TWIST (1838)

It was a nice sickly season just at this time. In commercial phrase, coffins were looking up.

APRIL 25
OUR MUTUAL FRIEND (1865)

"Are you thankful for not being young?"

"Yes, sir. If I was young, it would all have to be gone through again, and the end would be a weary way off, don't you see?"

APRIL 26
BLEAK HOUSE (1853)

"My son," said Mr. Turveydrop, "for those little points in which you are deficient—points of Deportment which are born with a man—which may be improved by cultivation, but can never be originated—you may still rely on me. I have been faithful to my post, since the days of His Royal Highness the Prince

Regent; and I will not desert it now. No, my son. If you have ever contemplated your father's poor position with a feeling of pride, you may rest assured that he will do nothing to tarnish it."

APRIL 27
OUR MUTUAL FRIEND (1865)

Mr. Podsnap's world was not a very large world, morally; no, nor even geographically: seeing that although his business was sustained upon commerce with other countries, he considered other countries, with that important reservation, a mistake, and of their manners and customs would conclusively observe, "Not English!" when, PRESTO! with a flourish of the arm and a flush of the face, they were swept away.

APRIL 28
DOMBEY AND SON (1848)

It being a part of Mrs. Pipchin's system not to encourage a child's mind to develop and expand itself like a young flower, but to open it by force like an oyster.

APRIL 29

THE PICKWICK PAPERS (1837)

"Did it ever strike you, on such a morning as this, that drowning would be happiness and peace?"

"God bless me, no!" replied Mr. Pickwick, edging a little from the balustrade, as the possibility of the dismal man's tipping him over by way of experiment, occurred to him rather forcibly.

APRIL 30

DAVID COPPERFIELD (1850)

But, sometimes, when I took [Dora] up, and felt that she was lighter in my arms, a dead blank feeling came upon me, as if I were approaching to some frozen region yet unseen, that numbed my life. I avoided the recognition of this feeling by any name, or by any communing with myself; until one night, when it was very strong upon me, and my aunt had left her with a parting cry of "Good night, Little Blossom," I sat down at my desk alone, and cried to think, Oh what a fatal name it was, and how the blossom withered in its bloom upon the tree!

MAY

The first of May! There is a merry freshness in the sound, calling to our minds a thousand thoughts of all that is pleasant in nature and beautiful in her most delightful form. What man is there, over whose mind a bright spring morning does not exercise a magic influence—carrying him back to the days of his childish sports, and conjuring up before him the old green field with its gently-waving trees, where the birds sang as he has never heard them since—where the butterfly fluttered far more gaily than he ever sees him now, in all his ramblings—where the sky seemed bluer, and the sun shone more brightly—where the air blew more freshly over greener grass, and sweeter-smelling flowers—where everything wore a richer and more brilliant hue than it is ever dressed in now! Such are the deep feelings of childhood, and such are the impressions which every lovely object stamps upon its heart!

"The First of May—Scenes,"
Sketches by Boz (1836)

MAY 1

The rapid and unbroken succession of novelties that had passed before me, came back like half-formed dreams; and a crowd of objects wandered in the greatest confusion through my mind, as I travelled on, by a solitary road. At intervals, some one among them would stop, as it were, in its restless flitting to and fro, and enable me to look at it, quite steadily, and behold it in full distinctness. After a few moments, it would dissolve, like a view in a magic-lantern; and while I saw some part of it quite plainly, and some faintly, and some not at all, would show me another of the many places I had lately seen, lingering behind it, and coming through it. This was no sooner visible than, in its turn, it melted into something else.

MAY 2

"Oh! The depressing institutions of that British empire, colonel!" said Jefferson Brick. "Master!"

"What's the matter with the word?" asked Martin.

"I should hope it was never heard in our country, sir: that's all," said Jefferson Brick: "except when it is used by some degraded Help, new to the blessings of our form of government as this Help is. There are no masters here."

"All 'owners,' are they?" said Martin.

MAY 3

BARNABY RUDGE (1841)

A mob is usually a creature of very mysterious existence, particularly in a large city. Where it comes from or whither it goes, few men can tell. Assembling and dispersing with equal suddenness, it is as difficult to follow to its various sources as the sea itself; nor does the parallel stop here, for the ocean is not more fickle and uncertain, more terrible when roused, more unreasonable, or more cruel.

MAY 4

OUR MUTUAL FRIEND (1865)

How the fascinating Tippins gets on when arraying herself for the bewilderment of the senses of men, is known only to the Graces and her maid; but perhaps even that engaging creature . . . could dispense with a good deal of the trouble attendant on the daily restoration of her charms, seeing that as to her face and neck this adorable divinity is, as it were, a diurnal species of lobster—throwing off a shell every forenoon, and needing to keep in a retired spot until the crust hardens.

MAY 5

"PREFACE" TO BLEAK HOUSE (1853)

A Chancery Judge once had the kindness to inform me, as one of a company . . . not labouring under any suspicion of lunacy, that the Court of Chancery, though the shining subject of much popular prejudice (at which point I thought the Judge's eye had a cast in my direction), was almost immaculate. . . .

This seemed to me too profound a joke to be inserted in the body of this book, or I should have restored it to Conversation Kenge or to Mr. Vholes, with one or the other of whom I think it must have originated.

MAY 6

A CHILD'S HISTORY OF ENGLAND (1852–54)

We now come to King Henry the Eighth, whom it has been too much the fashion to call "Bluff King Hal," and "Burly King Harry," and other fine names; but whom I shall take the liberty to call, plainly, one of the most detestable villains that ever drew breath.

"It was signed with an 'L' and eight stars, [said Mr. Leo Hunter] and appeared originally in a Lady's Magazine. It commenced

> 'Can I view thee panting, lying
> On thy stomach, without sighing;
> Can I unmoved see thee dying
>> On a log,
>> Expiring frog!'"

"Bcautiful!" said Mr. Pickwick.
"Fine," said Mr. Leo Hunter, "so simple."
"Very," said Mr. Pickwick.

MAY 8

LITTLE DORRIT (1857)

Mrs. Merdle was at home, and was in her nest of crimson and gold, with the parrot on a neighbouring stem watching her with his head on one side, as if he took her for another splendid parrot of a larger species.

My aunt mused a little while, and then said:

"Mr. Micawber, I wonder you have never turned your thoughts to emigration."

"Madam," returned Mr. Micawber, "it was the dream of my youth, and the fallacious aspiration of my riper years." I am thoroughly persuaded, by-the-bye, that he had never thought of it in his life.

MAY 10

THE OLD CURIOSITY SHOP (1841)

"Let us be beggars," said the child [Nell], passing an arm round his neck, "I have no fear but we shall have enough, I am sure we shall. Let us walk through country places, and sleep in fields and under trees, and never think of money again, or anything that can make you sad, but rest at nights, and have the sun and wind upon our faces in the day, and thank God together! Let us never set foot in dark rooms or melancholy houses, any more, but wander up and down wherever we like to go; and when you are tired, you shall stop to rest in the pleasantest place that we can find, and I will go and beg for both."

The child's voice was lost in sobs as she dropped upon the old man's neck; nor did she weep alone.

I wish some well-fed philosopher, whose meat and drink turn to gall within him; whose blood is ice, whose heart is iron; could have seen Oliver Twist clutching at the dainty viands that the dog had neglected. I wish he could have witnessed the horrible avidity with which Oliver tore the bits asunder with all the ferocity of famine. There is only one thing I should like better; and that would be to see the Philosopher making the same sort of meal himself, with the same relish.

"Where do you suppose . . . Mr. Crimple's stomach is?" [asked Dr. Jobling.]

Mr. Crimple . . . clapped his hand immediately below his waistcoat.

"Not at all," cried the doctor; "not at all. Quite a popular mistake! My good sir, you're altogether deceived."

"I feel it there, when it's out of order; that's all I know," said Crimple.

"You think you do," replied the doctor; "but science knows better. There was a patient of mine once . . . who was so overcome by the idea of having all his life laboured under an erroneous view of the locality of this important organ, that when I assured him, on my professional reputation, he was mistaken, he burst into tears, put out his hand, and said, 'Jobling, God bless you!' Immediately afterwards he became speechless, and was ultimately buried at Brixton."

MAY 13

"MRS. LIRRIPER'S LEGACY,"
CHRISTMAS STORIES (1864)

"Ah! It's pleasant to drop into my own easy-chair my dear though a little palpitating what with trotting upstairs and what with trotting down, and why kitchen stairs should all be corner stairs is for the builders to justify though I do not think they fully understand their trade and never did, else why the sameness and why not more conveniences and lower draughts and likewise making a practice of laying the plaster on too thick I am well convinced which holds the damp, and as to chimney-pots putting them on by guesswork like hats at a party and no more knowing what their effect will be upon the smoke bless you than I do if so much, except that it will mostly be either to send it down your throat in a straight form or give it a twist before it goes there."

There are very few moments in a man's existence when he experiences so much ludicrous distress, or meets with so little charitable commiseration, as when he is in pursuit of his own hat. A vast deal of coolness, and a peculiar degree of judgment, are requisite in catching a hat. A man must not be pre- cipitate, or he runs over it; he must not rush into the opposite extreme, or he loses it altogether. The best way is, to keep gently up with the object of pursuit, to be wary and cautious, to watch your opportunity well, get gradually before it, then make a rapid dive, seize it by the crown, and stick it firmly on your head: smiling pleasantly all the time, as if you thought it as good a joke as anybody else.

I must confess, without any disguise, that the preva- lence of those two odious practices of chewing and expectorating began about this time to be anything but agreeable, and soon became most offensive and sickening. In all the public places of America, this filthy custom is recognised. In the courts of law, the judge has his spittoon, the crier his, the witness his, and the prisoner his; while the jurymen and spectators are provided for, as so many men who in the course of nature must desire to spit incessantly.

MAY 16

DOMBEY AND SON (1848)

"Do you think [Florence] could—you know—eh?"

"I beg your pardon, Mr. Toots," said Susan, "but I don't hear you."

"Do you think she could be brought, you know—not exactly at once, but in time—in a long time—to—to love me, you know? There!" said poor Mr. Toots.

"Oh dear no!" returned Susan, shaking her head. "I should say, never. Ne-ver!"

"Thank'ee!" said Mr. Toots. "It's of no consequence. Good night. It's of no consequence, thank'ee!"

MAY 17

MARTIN CHUZZLEWIT (1844)

Then there was a young gentleman, grand-nephew of Mr. Martin Chuzzlewit, very dark and very hairy, and apparently born for no particular purpose but to save looking-glasses the trouble of reflecting more than just the first idea and sketchy notion of a face, which had never been carried out. Then there was a solitary female cousin who was remarkable for nothing but being very deaf, and living by herself, and always having the tooth-ache. Then there was George Chuzzlewit, a gay bachelor cousin, who claimed to be young but had been younger, and was inclined to corpulency, and rather over-fed himself: to that extent, indeed, that his eyes were strained in their sockets, as if with constant surprise. . . . Last of all there were present Mr. Chevy Slime and his friend Tigg. And it is worthy of remark, that although each person present disliked the other, mainly because he or she *did* belong to the family, they one and all concurred in hating Mr. Tigg because he didn't.

MAY 18

A CHILD'S HISTORY OF ENGLAND (1852–54)

War is a dreadful thing; and it is appalling to know how the English were obliged, next morning, to kill those prisoners mortally wounded, who yet writhed in agony upon the ground; how the dead upon the French side were stripped by their own countrymen and countrywomen, and afterwards buried in great pits; how the dead upon the English side were piled up in a great barn, and how their bodies and the barn were all burned together. It is in such things, and in many more much too horrible to relate, that the real desolation and wickedness of war consist.

[On a public beheading in Rome:] He [the prisoner] immediately kneeled down, below the knife. His neck fitting into a hole, made for the purpose, in a cross plank, was shut down, by another plank above; exactly like the pillory. Immediately below him was a leathern bag. And into it his head rolled instantly.

The executioner was holding it by the hair, and walking with it round the scaffold, showing it to the people, before one quite knew that the knife had fallen heavily, and with a rattling sound.

MAY 20
HARD TIMES (1854)

"Now, what I want is, Facts. Teach these boys and girls nothing but Facts. Facts alone are wanted in life. Plant nothing else, and root out everything else. You can only form the minds of reasoning animals upon Facts: nothing else will ever be of any service to them. This is the principle on which I bring up my own children, and this is the principle on which I bring up these children. Stick to Facts, Sir!"

Again. Is it necessary or advisable [for preachers] to address such an audience continually as "fellow-sinners"? Is it not enough to be fellow-creatures, born yesterday, suffering and striving to-day, dying to-morrow? By our common humanity, my brothers and sisters, by our common capacities for pain and pleasure, by our common laughter and our common tears.

MAY 22

GREAT EXPECTATIONS (1861)

MY DEAR MR. PIP,

I write this by request of Mr. Gargery, for to let you know that he is going to London in company with Mr. Wopsle and would be glad if agreeable to be allowed to see you. He would call at Barnard's Hotel Tuesday morning at nine o'clock, when if not agreeable please leave word. Your poor sister is much the same as when you left. We talk of you in the kitchen every night, and wonder what you are saying and doing. If now considered in the light of a liberty, excuse it for the love of poor old days. No more, dear Mr. Pip, from

Your ever obliged, and affectionate servant,
BIDDY

P.S. He wishes me most particular to write what larks. *He says you will understand. I hope and do not doubt it will be agreeable to see him even though a gentleman, for you had ever a good heart, and he is a worthy worthy man. I have read him all excepting only the last little sentence, and he wishes me most particular to write again* what larks.

MAY 23

THE OLD CURIOSITY SHOP (1841)

For she was dead. There, upon her little bed, she lay at rest. The solemn stillness was no marvel now.

She was dead. No sleep so beautiful and calm, so free from trace of pain, so fair to look upon. She seemed a creature fresh from the hand of God, and waiting for the breath of life; not one who had lived and suffered death.

Her couch was dressed with here and there some winter berries and green leaves, gathered in a spot she had been used to favour. "When I die, put me near something that has loved the light, and had the sky above it always." Those were her words.

She was dead. Dear, gentle, patient, noble Nell was dead. Her little bird—a poor slight thing the pressure of a finger would have crushed—was stirring nimbly in its cage; and the strong heart of its child-mistress was mute and motionless for ever.

MAY 24

P.S.—I open this note to say we have just discovered the cause of little Frederick's restlessness. It is not fever, as I apprehended, but a small pin, which nurse accidentally stuck in his leg yesterday evening. We have taken it out, and he appears more composed, though he still sobs a good deal.

MAY 25

LITTLE DORRIT (1857)

"Mr. Merdle is dead" [said Physician].

"I should wish," said the Chief Butler, "to give a month's notice."

"Mr. Merdle has destroyed himself."

"Sir," said the Chief Butler, "that is very unpleasant to the feelings of one in my position, as calculated to awaken prejudice; and I should wish to leave immediately."

MAY 26

GREAT EXPECTATIONS (1861)

"Now, I ain't alone, as you may think I am" [said the convict]. "There's a young man hid with me, in comparison with which young man I am a Angel. That young man hears the words I speak. That young man has a secret way pecooliar to himself, of getting at a boy, and at his heart, and at his liver. It is in wain for a boy to attempt to hide himself from that young man. A boy may lock his door, may be warm in bed, may tuck himself up, may draw the clothes over his head, may think himself comfortable and safe, but that young man will softly creep and creep his way to him and tear him open. I am akeeping that young man from harming of you at the present moment, with great difficulty. I find it wery hard to hold that young man off of your inside. Now, what do you say?"

MAY 27

NICHOLAS NICKLEBY (1839)

"I really don't know, I do *not* know what's to be done with that young fellow; he's always a-wishing something horrid. He said, once, he wished he was a donkey, because then he wouldn't have a father as didn't love him! Pretty wicious that for a child of six!"

Mr. Squeers was so much moved by the contemplation of this hardened nature in one so young, that he angrily put up the letter.

MAY 28
MARTIN CHUZZLEWIT (1844)

"That's a woman [Mrs. Gamp] who observes and reflects in an uncommon manner. She's the sort of woman, now," said Mould, . . . "one would almost feel disposed to bury for nothing: and do it neatly, too!"

MAY 29
"PREFACE" TO BLEAK HOUSE (1853)

Another case [of spontaneous combustion], very clearly described by a dentist, occurred at the town of Columbus, in the United States of America, quite recently. The subject was a German, who kept a liquor-shop, and was an inveterate drunkard.

MAY 30
OLIVER TWIST (1838)

"Fagin," said the jailer.

"That's me!" cried [Fagin], falling, instantly, into the attitude of listening he had assumed upon his trial. "An old man, my Lord; a very old, old man!"

"Here," said the turnkey, laying his hand upon his breast to keep him down. "Here's somebody wants to see you. . . . Fagin, Fagin! Are you a man?"

"I shan't be one long," he replied, looking up

with a face retaining no human expression but rage and terror. "Strike them all dead! What right have they to butcher me?"

MAY 31

GREAT EXPECTATIONS (1861)

That was a memorable day to me, for it made great changes in me. But it is the same with any life. Imagine one selected day struck out of it, and think how different its course would have been. Pause you who read this, and think for a moment of the long chain of iron or gold, of thorns or flowers, that would never have bound you, but for the formation of the first link on one memorable day.

JUNE

Oh! how some of those idle fellows longed to be outside, and how they looked at the open door and window, as if they half meditated rushing violently out, plunging into the woods, and being wild boys and savages from that time forth. What rebellious thoughts of the cool river, and some shady bathing-place beneath willow trees with branches dipping in the water, kept tempting and urging that sturdy boy, who, with his shirt-collar unbuttoned and flung back as far as it could go, sat fanning his flushed face with a spelling-book, wishing himself a whale, or a tittlebat, or a fly, or anything but a boy at school on that hot, broiling day! Heat! ask that other boy, whose seat being nearest to the door gave him opportunities of gliding out into the garden and driving his companions to madness by dipping his face into the bucket of the well and then rolling on the grass—ask him if there were ever such a day as that, when even the bees were diving deep down into the cups of flowers and stopping there, as if they had made up their minds to retire from business and be manufacturers of honey no more. The day was made for laziness, and lying on one's back in green places, and staring at the sky till its brightness forced one to shut one's eyes and go to sleep; and was this a time to be poring over musty books in a dark room, slighted by the very sun itself? Monstrous!

The Old Curiosity Shop (1841)

JUNE 1

THE OLD CURIOSITY SHOP (1841)

"It's not a common offer, bear in mind," said [Mrs. Jarley], rising into the tone and manner in which she was accustomed to address her audiences; "it's Jarley's wax-work, remember. The duty's very light and genteel, the company particularly select, the exhibition takes place in assembly-rooms, town-halls, large rooms at inns, or auction-galleries. There is none of your open-air wagrancy at Jarley's, recollect; there is no tarpaulin and sawdust at Jarlcy's, remember. Every expectation held out in the hand-bills is realised to the utmost, and the whole forms an effect of imposing brilliancy hitherto unrivalled in this kingdom. Remember that the price of admission is only sixpence, and that this is an opportunity which may never occur again!"

JUNE 2

MARTIN CHUZZLEWIT (1844)

"Bless you," said Mark, "I know [the slave's story is true]. . . . That master died; so did his second master from having his head cut open with a hatchet by another slave, who, when he'd done it, went and drowned himself: then he got a better one. In years and years he saved up a little money, and bought his freedom, which he got pretty cheap at last, on account of his strength being nearly gone, and he being ill. Then he come here. And now he's a-saving up to treat himself, afore he dies, to one small purchase; it's nothing to speak of; only his own daughter; that's all!" cried Mr. Tapley, becoming excited. "Liberty for ever! Hurrah! Hail, Columbia!"

JUNE 3

THE OLD CURIOSITY SHOP (1841)

The boy sulkily complied, muttering at first, but desisting when he looked round and saw that Quilp was following him with a steady look. And here it may be remarked, that between this boy and the dwarf there existed a strange kind of mutual liking. How born or bred, or how nourished upon blows and threats on one side, and retorts and defiances on the other, is not to the purpose. Quilp would certainly suffer nobody to contradict him but the boy, and the boy would assuredly not have submitted to be so knocked about by anybody but Quilp, when he had the power to run away at any time he chose.

"Now," said Quilp . . . . "Stand upon your head again, and I'll cut one of your feet off."

The boy made no answer, but directly Quilp had shut himself in, stood on his head before the door, then walked on his hands to the back and stood on his head there, and then to the opposite side and repeated the performance.

JUNE 4

[Dickens] seems almost as unstable as Dostoevsky. He was capable of great hardness and cruelty, and not merely toward those whom he had cause to resent: people who patronized or intruded on him. On one occasion, in the presence of other guests, he ordered Forster out of his house over some discussion that had arisen at dinner; and his treatment of Mrs. Dickens suggests . . . the behavior of a Renaissance monarch summarily consigning to a convent the wife who had served her turn. There is more of emotional reality behind Quilp in "The Old Curiosity Shop" than there is behind Little Nell. If Little Nell sounds bathetic today, Quilp has lost none of his fascination. He is ugly, malevolent, perverse; he delights in making mischief for its own sake, yet he exercises over the members of his household a power which is almost an attraction and which resembles what was known in Dickens' day as "malicious animal magnetism." Though Quilp is ceaselessly tormenting his wife and browbeating the boy who works for him, they never attempt to escape: they admire him; in a sense they love him.

JUNE 5

As for the children of the [Wilfer] union, their experience of these [anniversary] festivals had been sufficiently uncomfortable to lead them annually to wish, when out of their tenderest years, either that Ma had married somebody else instead of much-teased Pa, or that Pa had married somebody else instead of Ma.

JUNE 6

"DOCTOR MARIGOLD," CHRISTMAS STORIES (1865)

I am a Cheap Jack, and my father's name was Willum Marigold. It was in his lifetime supposed by some that his name was William, but my own father always consistently said, No, it was Willum. On which point I content myself with looking at the argument this way: If a man is not allowed to know his own name in a free country, how much is he allowed to know in a land of slavery?

JUNE 7

AMERICAN NOTES (1842)

Cant as we may, and as we shall to the end of all things, it is very much harder for the poor to be virtuous than it is for the rich; and the good that is in them, shines the brighter for it.

JUNE 8
OLIVER TWIST (1838)

"The prices allowed by the board are very small, Mr. Bumble."

"So are the coffins," replied the beadle: with precisely as near an approach to a laugh as a great official ought to indulge in.

Mr. Sowerberry was much tickled at this: as of course he ought to be; and laughed a long time without cessation. "Well, well, Mr. Bumble," he said at length, "there's no denying that, since the new system of feeding has come in, the coffins are something narrower and more shallow than they used to be; but we must have some profit, Mr. Bumble."

JUNE 9
LITTLE DORRIT (1857)

It was one of those summer evenings when there is no greater darkness than a long twilight. The vista of street and bridge was plain to see, and the sky was serene and beautiful. People stood and sat at their doors, playing with children and enjoying the

evening; numbers were walking for air; the worry of
the day had almost worried itself out.

JUNE 10

LONDON TIMES, OBITUARY, FRIDAY, JUNE 10, 1870

One whom young and old, wherever the English language is spoken, have been accustomed to regard as
a personal friend, is suddenly taken away from us.
Charles Dickens is no more.

JUNE 11

THE PICKWICK PAPERS (1837)

This constant succession of glasses produced considerable effect upon Mr. Pickwick; his countenance
beamed with the most sunny smiles, laughter
played around his lips, and good-humoured merriment twinkled in his eye. Yielding by degrees to
the influence of the exciting liquid, rendered more
so by the heat, Mr. Pickwick expressed a strong desire to recollect a song which he had heard in his
infancy, and the attempt proving abortive, sought to
stimulate his memory with more glasses of punch,
which appeared to have quite a contrary effect; for,
from forgetting the words of the song, he began to
forget how to articulate any words at all; and finally,

after rising to his legs to address the company in an eloquent speech, he fell into the barrow, and fast asleep, simultaneously.

JUNE 12

"THE LADIES' SOCIETIES—OUR PARISH," SKETCHES BY BOZ (1836)

[T]he orator (an Irishman) came. He talked of green isles—other shores—vast Atlantic—bosom of the deep—Christian charity—blood and extermination —mercy in hearts—arms in hands—altars and homes—household gods. He wiped his eyes, he blew his nose, and he quoted Latin. The effect was tremendous—the Latin was a decided hit.

JUNE 13

BARNABY RUDGE (1841)

"It'll clear at eleven o'clock" [said John Willet]. "No sooner and no later. Not before and not arterwards."

"How do you make that out?" said a little man in the opposite corner. "The moon is past the full, and she rises at nine."

John looked sedately and solemnly at his questioner until he had brought his mind to bear upon the whole of his observation, and then made answer, in a tone which seemed to imply that the moon was peculiarly his business and nobody else's:

"Never you mind about the moon. Don't you trouble yourself about her. You let the moon alone, and I'll let you alone."

"No offence I hope?" said the little man.

Again John waited leisurely until the observation had thoroughly penetrated to his brain, and then replying, "No offence *as yet*," applied a light to his pipe and smoked in placid silence.

JUNE 14

DOMBEY AND SON (1848)

"Wal'r, my boy," replied the Captain [Cuttle], "in the Proverbs of Solomon you will find the following words, 'May we never want a friend in need, nor a bottle to give him!' When found, make a note of."

JUNE 15

GREAT EXPECTATIONS (1861)

"[I know you would not join in a hunt to trap a] wretched warmint, hunted as near death and dung-hill as this poor wretched warmint is!"

Something clicked in his throat as if he had works in him like a clock, and was going to strike. And he smeared his ragged rough sleeve over his eyes.

Pitying [the convict's] desolation, and watching him as he gradually settled down upon the pie, I made bold to say, "I am glad you enjoy it."

"Did you speak?"

"I said, I was glad you enjoyed it."

"Thankee, my boy. I do."

JUNE 16

OUR MUTUAL FRIEND (1865)

"Oh dear me, dear me!" sighs Mr. Venus, heavily, snuffing the candle, "the world that appeared so flowery has ceased to blow! You're casting your eye round the shop, Mr. Wegg. Let me show you a light. My working bench. My young man's bench. A Wice. Tools. Bones, warious. Skulls, warious. Preserved Indian baby. African ditto. Bottled preparations, warious. Everything within reach of your hand, in good preservation. The mouldy ones a-top. What's in those hampers over them again, I don't quite remember. Say, human warious. Cats. Articulated English baby. Dogs. Ducks. Glass eyes, warious. Mummied bird. Dried cuticle, warious. Oh dear me! That's the general panoramic view." . . . .

"Where am I [i.e., my leg]?" asks Mr. Wegg.

"You're somewhere in the back shop across the yard, sir; and speaking quite candidly, I wish I'd never bought you of the Hospital Porter."

"Mother will be proud, indeed," he said, as we walked away together. "Or she would be proud, if it wasn't sinful, Master Copperfield."

"Yet you didn't mind supposing *I* was proud this morning," I returned.

"Oh dear, no, Master Copperfield!" returned Uriah. "Oh, believe me, no! Such a thought never came into my head! I shouldn't have deemed it at all proud if you had thought *us* too umble for you. Because we are so very umble."

JUNE 18
HARD TIMES (1854)

Thomas Gradgrind, Sir. A man of realities. A man of facts and calculations. A man who proceeds upon the principle that two and two are four, and nothing over, and who is not to be talked into allowing for anything over. . . . With a rule and a pair of scales, and the multiplication table always in his pocket, Sir, ready to weigh and measure any parcel of human nature, and tell you exactly what it comes to.

JUNE 19

LITTLE DORRIT (1857)

"But if we talk of not having changed," said Flora, who, whatever she said, never once came to a full stop, "look at Papa, is not Papa precisely what he was when you went away, isn't it cruel and unnatural of Papa to be such a reproach to his own child, if we go on in this way much longer people who don't know us will begin to suppose that I am Papa's Mama!"

JUNE 20

BLEAK HOUSE (1853)

There has been only one child in the Smallweed family for several generations. Little old men and women there have been, but no child, until Mr. Smallweed's grandmother, now living, became weak in her intellect, and fell (for the first time) into a childish state. With such infantine graces as a total want of observation, memory, understanding and interest, and an eternal disposition to fall asleep over the fire and into it, Mr. Smallweed's grandmother has undoubtedly brightened the family.

JUNE 21
T. S. ELIOT, ON DICKENS (1927)

Dickens's figures belong to poetry, like the figures of Dante or Shakespeare, in that a single phrase, either by them or about them, may be enough to set them wholly before us.

JUNE 22
AMERICAN NOTES (1842)

Whatever the defects of American universities may be, they disseminate no prejudices; rear no bigots; dig up the buried ashes of no old superstitions; never interpose between the people and their improvement; exclude no man because of his religious opinions; above all, in their whole course of study and instruction, recognise a world, and a broad one too, lying beyond the college walls.

JUNE 23
LITTLE DORRIT (1857)

Mrs. General was not to be told of anything shocking. Accidents, miseries, and offences, were never to be mentioned before her. Passion was to go to sleep in the presence of Mrs. General, and blood was to change to milk and water. The little that was left in the world, when all these deductions were made, it was Mrs. General's province to varnish. In that formation process of hers, she dipped the smallest of brushes into the largest of pots, and varnished the surface of every object that came under consideration. The more cracked it was, the more Mrs. General varnished it.

JUNE 24

BLEAK HOUSE (1853)

England has been in a dreadful state for some weeks. Lord Coodle would go out, Sir Thomas Doodle wouldn't come in, and there being nobody in Great Britain (to speak of) except Coodle and Doodle, there has been no Government.

JUNE 25

GEORGE BERNARD SHAW ON LITTLE DORRIT (1937)

Little Dorrit is a more seditious book than *Das Kapital*. All over Europe men and women are in prison for pamphlets and speeches which are to *Little Dorrit* as red pepper is to dynamite.

JUNE 26

MARTIN CHUZZLEWIT (1844)

Mr. Bailey had a great opinion of [his horse]. . . .
But he never told him so. On the contrary, it was his
practice, in driving that animal, to assail him with
disrespectful, if not injurious, expressions, as, "Ah!
would you!" "Did you think it, then?" "Where are
you going to now?" "No, you won't, my lad!" and
similar fragmentary remarks.

JUNE 27

THE OLD CURIOSITY SHOP (1841)

By a like pleasant fiction [Mr. Swiveller's] single
chamber was always mentioned in the plural number. In its disengaged times, the tobacconist had
announced it in his window as "apartments" for a
single gentleman, and Mr. Swiveller, following up
the hint, never failed to speak of it as his rooms, his
lodgings, or his chambers: conveying to his hearers a notion of indefinite space, and leaving their
imaginations to wander through long suites of lofty
halls, at pleasure.

. . . To be the friend of Swiveller you must reject
all circumstantial evidence, all reason, observation,
and experience.

JUNE 28

"I sold myself," said Mr. Bumble, pursuing the same train of reflection, "for six teaspoons, a pair of sugar-tongs, and a milk-pot; with a small quantity of second-hand furniture, and twenty pound in money. I went very reasonable. Cheap, dirt cheap!"

"Cheap!" cried a shrill voice in Mr. Bumble's ear: "you would have been dear at any price; and dear enough I paid for you, Lord above knows that!"

JUNE 29

THE MYSTERY OF EDWIN DROOD (1870)

But Rosa soon made the discovery that Miss Twinkleton didn't read fairly. She cut the love-scenes, interpolated passages in praise of female celibacy, and was guilty of other glaring pious frauds.

JUNE 30

BARNABY RUDGE (1841)

Mrs. Varden was a lady of what is commonly called an uncertain temper—a phrase which being interpreted signifies a temper tolerably certain to make everybody more or less uncomfortable. Thus it generally happened, that when other people were merry, Mrs. Varden was dull; and that when other people were dull, Mrs. Varden was disposed to be amazingly cheerful.

JULY

It was one of those hot, silent nights, when people sit at windows listening for the thunder which they know will shortly break; when they recall dismal tales of hurricanes and earthquakes; and of lonely travellers on open plains, and lonely ships at sea, struck by lightning. Lightning flashed and quivered on the black horizon even now; and hollow murmurings were in the wind, as though it had been blowing where the thunder rolled, and still was charged with its exhausted echoes. But the storm, though gathering swiftly, had not yet come up; and the prevailing stillness was the more solemn, from the dull intelligence that seemed to hover in the air, of noise and conflict afar off.

Martin Chuzzlewit (1844)

Mr. and Mrs. Veneering were bran-new people in a bran-new house in a bran-new quarter of London. Everything about the Veneerings was spick and span new. All their furniture was new, all their friends were new, all their servants were new, their plate was new, their carriage was new, their harness was new, their horses were new, their pictures were new, they themselves were new, they were as newly married as was lawfully compatible with their having a bran-new baby.

JULY 2
MARTIN CHUZZLEWIT (1844)

"You have become indifferent since then, I suppose?" said Mr. Pecksniff. "Use is second nature, Mrs. Gamp."

"You may well say second natur, sir," returned that lady. "One's first ways is to find sich things a trial to the feelings, and so is one's lasting custom. If it wasn't for the nerve a little sip of liquor gives me (I never was able to do more than taste it), I never could go through with what I sometimes has to do. 'Mrs. Harris,' I says, at the very last case as ever I acted in, which it was but a young person, 'Mrs. Harris,' I says, 'leave the bottle on the chimley-piece, and don't ask me to take none, but let me put my lips to it when I am so dispoged, and then I will do what I am engaged to do, according to the best of my ability. 'Mrs. Gamp,' she says, in answer, 'if ever there was a sober creetur to be got at eighteen pence a day for working people, and three and six for gentlefolks—night watching,' said Mrs. Gamp, with emphasis, 'being a extra charge—you are that inwallable person.' 'Mrs. Harris,' I says to her, 'don't name the charge, for if I could afford to lay all my feller creeturs out for nothink, I would gladly do it, sich is the love I bears 'em.'"

JULY 3
GREAT EXPECTATIONS (1861)

The Educational scheme or Course established by Mr. Wopsle's great-aunt may be resolved into the following synopsis. The pupils ate apples and put straws down one another's backs, until Mr. Wopsle's great-aunt collected her energies, and made an indiscriminate totter at them with a birch-rod.

JULY 4
BLEAK HOUSE (1853)

"It is," says Chadband, "the ray of rays, the sun of suns, the moon of moons, the star of stars. It is the light of Terewth."

JULY 5
"NURSE'S STORIES,"
THE UNCOMMERCIAL TRAVELLER (1860)

The first diabolical character who intruded himself on my peaceful youth . . . was a certain Captain Murderer. . . . Captain Murderer's mission was matrimony, and the gratification of a cannibal appetite with tender brides. . . .

The young woman who brought me acquainted with Captain Murderer had a fiendish enjoyment of my terrors, and used to begin, I remember—as a sort of introductory overture—by clawing the air with both hands, and uttering a long low hollow groan. So acutely did I suffer from this ceremony in combination with this infernal Captain, that I sometimes used to plead I thought I was hardly strong enough and old enough to hear the story again just yet.

JULY 6

"Was there ever," cried Mr. Tigg, . . . "such an independent spirit as is possessed by that extraordinary creature? Was there ever such a Roman as our friend Chiv? Was there ever a man of such a purely classical turn of thought, and of such a toga-like simplicity of nature? Was there ever a man with such a flow of eloquence? Might he not . . . have sat upon a tripod in the ancient times, and prophesied to a perfectly unlimited extent, if previously supplied with gin-and-water at the public cost?"

JULY 7

Here [on Broadway in New York City] is a solitary swine lounging homeward by himself. He has only one ear; having parted with the other to vagrant-dogs in the course of his city rambles. But he gets on very well without it; and leads a roving, gentlemanly, vagabond kind of life, somewhat answering to that of our club-men at home.

THE OLD CURIOSITY SHOP (1841)

The throng of people hurried by, in two opposite streams, with no symptom of cessation or exhaustion; intent upon their own affairs; and undisturbed in their business speculations, by the roar of carts and waggons laden with clashing wares, the slipping of horses' feet upon the wet and greasy pavement, the rattling of the rain on windows and umbrella-tops, the jostling of the more impatient passengers, and all the noise and tumult of a crowded street in the high tide of its occupation: while the two poor strangers, [Nell and her grandfather,] stunned, and bewildered by the hurry they beheld but had no part in, looked mournfully on; feeling, amidst the crowd, a solitude which has no parallel but in the thirst of the shipwrecked mariner, who, tost to and fro upon the billows of a mighty ocean, his red eyes blinded by looking on the water which hems him in on every side, has not one drop to cool his burning tongue.

JULY 9

DAVID COPPERFIELD (1850)

Why do I secretly give Miss Shepherd twelve Brazil nuts for a present, I wonder? They are not expressive of affection, they are difficult to pack into a parcel of any regular shape, they are hard to crack, even in room doors, and they are oily when cracked; yet I feel that they are appropriate to Miss Shepherd. Soft, seedy biscuits, also, I bestow upon Miss Shepherd; and oranges innumerable. Once, I kiss Miss Shepherd in the cloak room. Ecstasy!

JULY 10
MARTIN CHUZZLEWIT (1844)

M. Todgers was a lady, rather a bony and hard-featured lady, with a row of curls in front of her head, shaped like little barrels of beer; and on the top of it something made of net—you couldn't call it a cap exactly—which looked like a black cobweb.

JULY 11
HARD TIMES (1854)

"Now, you know," said Mr. Bounderby [to Stephen], taking some sherry, "we have never had any difficulty with you. . . . You don't expect to be set up in a coach and six, and to be fed on turtle soup and venison, with a gold spoon, as a good many of 'em do!"

JULY 12

As to the suffrage, I have lost hope even in the Ballot. We appear to me to have proved the failure of Representative Institutions, without an educated and advanced people to support them. What with teaching people to "keep in their stations"—what with bringing up the Soul and Body of the land to be a good child, or to go to the Beershop, to go a-poaching and go to the devil—what with having no such thing as a Middle Class (. . . but a poor fringe on the mantle of the Upper)—what with flunkeyism, toadyism . . . I do reluctantly believe that the English people are, habitually, consenting parties to the miserable imbecility into which we have fallen, and never *will help themselves out of it*. Who is to do it, if anybody is, God knows. But at present we are on the down-hill road to being conquered, and the people *will* be content to hear incapable and insolent Premiers sing "Rule Britania," and *will not* be saved.

JULY 13

I have always noticed a prevalent want of courage, even among persons of superior intelligence and culture, as to imparting their own psychological experiences when those have been of a strange sort.

Almost all men are afraid that what they could relate in such wise would find no parallel or response in a listener's internal life, and might be suspected or laughed at.

JULY 14

"SCENES—SHOPS AND THEIR TENANTS," SKETCHES BY BOZ (1836)

What inexhaustible food for speculation do the streets of London afford! . . . [W]e have not the slightest commiseration for the man who can take up his hat and stick, and walk from Covent Garden to St. Paul's Churchyard, and back into the bargain, without deriving some amusement—we had almost said instruction—from his perambulation.

JULY 15

A CHILD'S HISTORY OF ENGLAND (1852–54)

All the Crusaders were not zealous Christians. Among them were vast numbers of the restless, idle, profligate, and adventurous spirits of the time. Some became Crusaders for the love of change; some, in the hope of plunder; some, because they had nothing to do at home; some, because they did what the priests told them; some, because they liked to see foreign countries; some, because they were fond of knocking men about, and would as soon knock a Turk about as a Christian.

JULY 16

LITTLE DORRIT (1857)

There was the dreary Sunday of [Arthur Clennam's] childhood, when he sat with his hands before him, scared out of his senses by a horrible tract which commenced business with the poor child by asking him in its title, why he was going to Perdition?—a piece of curiosity that he really in a frock and drawers was not in a condition to satisfy—and which, for the further attraction of his infant mind, had a parenthesis in every other line with some such hiccupping reference as 2 Ep. Thess. c. iii. v. 6&7.

JULY 17

MASTER HUMPHREY'S CLOCK (1840–41)

Solitary men are accustomed, I suppose, unconsciously to look upon solitude as their own peculiar property.

JULY 18

GREAT EXPECTATIONS (1861)

"Yes, Pip, dear boy," [said Magwitch,] "I've made a gentleman on you! It's me wot has done it! I swore that time, sure as ever I earned a guinea, that guinea should go to you. I swore arterwards, sure as ever I spec'lated and got rich, you should get rich. I lived rough, that you should live smooth; I worked hard that you should be above work. What odds, dear boy? Do I tell it fur you to feel a obligation? Not a bit. I tell it, fur you to know as that there hunted dung-hill dog wot you kep life in, got his head so high that he could make a gentleman—and, Pip, you're him!"

JULY 19

DAVID COPPERFIELD (1850)

The days [at Yarmouth] sported by us, as if Time had not grown up himself yet, but were a child too, and always at play. I told Em'ly I adored her, and that unless she confessed she adored me I should be reduced to the necessity of killing myself with a sword. She said she did, and I have no doubt she did.

Not that I have any curiosity to hear powerful preach-
ers. Time was, when I was dragged by the hair of my
head, as one may say, to hear too many. On summer evenings, when every flower, and tree, and bird,
might have better addressed my soft young heart, I
have in my day been caught in the palm of a female
hand by the crown, have been violently scrubbed
from the neck to the roots of the hair as a purifica-
tion for the Temple, and have then been carried off
highly charged with saponaceous electricity, to be
steamed like a potato in the unventilated breath of
the powerful Boanerges Boiler and his congregation,
until what small mind I had, was quite steamed out
of me.

"The family name" [said Tony Weller] "depends wery
much upon you, Samivel, and I hope you'll do wot's
right by it. Upon all little pints o' breedin', I know I
may trust you as vell as if it was my own self. So I've
only this here one little bit of adwice to give you. If
ever you gets to up'ards o' fifty, and feels disposed
to go amarryin' anybody—no matter who—jist you
shut yourself in your own room, if you've got one,

and pison yourself off hand. Hangin's wulgar, so don't you have nothin' to say to that. Pison yourself, Samivel my boy, pison yourself, and you'll be glad on it arterwards."

JULY 22

LITTLE DORRIT (1857)

"The Circumlocution Department," said Mr. Barnacle, "is not responsible for any gentleman's assumptions."

"May I inquire how I can obtain official information as to the real state of the case?"

"It is competent," said Mr. Barnacle, "to any member of the—Public," mentioning that obscure body with reluctance, as his natural enemy, "to memorialise the Circumlocution Department. Such formalities as are required to be observed in so doing, may be known on application to the proper branch of that Department."

JULY 23

THE OLD CURIOSITY SHOP (1841)

"I hate your virtuous people!" said the dwarf, throwing off a bumper of brandy, and smacking his lips, "ah! I hate 'em every one!"

JULY 24

GREAT EXPECTATIONS (1861)

"Let me see you play cards with this boy."

"With this boy! Why, he is a common labouring-boy!"

I thought I overheard Miss Havisham answer—only it seemed so unlikely—"Well? You can break his heart."

"What do you play, boy?" asked Estella of myself, with the greatest disdain.

"Nothing but beggar my neighbour, Miss."

"Beggar him," said Miss Havisham to Estella. So we sat down to cards.

JULY 25

MARTIN CHUZZLEWIT (1844)

[G]o, Teachers of content and honest pride, into the mine, the mill, the forge, the squalid depths of deepest ignorance, and uttermost abyss of man's neglect, and say can any hopeful plant spring up in air so foul that it extinguishes the soul's bright torch as fast as it is kindled! And, oh! ye Pharisees of the nineteen hundredth year of Christian Knowledge, who soundingly appeal to human nature, see first that it be human. Take heed it has not been transformed, during your slumber and the sleep of generations, into the nature of the Beasts.

JULY 26

Mr. Squeers's appearance was not prepossessing. He had but one eye, and the popular prejudice runs in favour of two. The eye he had was unquestionably useful, but decidedly not ornamental: being of a greenish grey, and in shape resembling the fanlight of a street door. The blank side of his face was much wrinkled and puckered up, which gave him a very sinister appearance, especially when he smiled, at which times his expression bordered closely on the villainous.

JULY 27

"Jo, can you say what I say?"

"I'll say anythink as you say, sir, fur I knows it's good."

"OUR FATHER."

"Our Father!—yes, that's wery good, sir."

"WHICH ART IN HEAVEN."

"Art in Heaven—is the light a-comin, sir?"

"It is close at hand. HALLOWED BE THY NAME!"

"Hallowed be—thy—"

The light is come upon the dark benighted way. Dead!

Dead, your Majesty. Dead, my lords and gentlemen. Dead, Right Reverends and Wrong Reverends of every order. Dead, men and women, born with Heavenly compassion in your hearts. And dying thus around us every day.

JULY 28
THE OLD CURIOSITY SHOP (1841)

[Quilp] staggered and fell—and next moment was fighting with the cold dark water!

. . . [Help was] close at hand, but could not make an effort to save him; . . . he himself had shut and barred them out. He answered the shout—with a yell, which seemed to make the hundred fires that danced before his eyes tremble and flicker, as if a gust of wind had stirred them. It was of no avail. The strong tide filled his throat, and bore him on, upon its rapid current.

Another mortal struggle, and he was up again, beating the water with his hands, and looking out, with wild and glaring eyes that showed him some black object he was drifting close upon. The hull of a ship! He could touch its smooth and slippery surface with his hand. One loud cry, now—but the resistless water bore him down before he could give it utterance, and, driving him under it, carried away a corpse.

JULY 29

King Richard . . . was a strong restless burly man, with one idea always in his head, and that the very troublesome idea of breaking the heads of other men.

JULY 30

GREAT EXPECTATIONS (1861)

"Pocket-handkerchiefs out, all!" cried Mr. Trabb at this point, in a depressed business-like voice— "Pocket-handkerchiefs out! We are ready!"

So, we all put our pocket-handkerchiefs to our faces, as if our noses were bleeding, and filed out two and two; Joe and I; Biddy and Pumblechook; Mr. and Mrs. Hubble. The remains of my poor sister had been brought round by the kitchen door, and, it being a point of Undertaking ceremony that the six bearers must be stifled and blinded under a horrible black velvet housing with a white border, the whole looked like a blind monster with twelve human legs, shuffling and blundering along under the guidance of two keepers—the postboy and his comrade.

One very striking thing about Dickens, especially considering the time he lived in, is his lack of vulgar nationalism. . . .

. . . [That lack] is in part the mark of a real largeness of mind, and in part results from his negative, rather unhelpful political attitude.

AUGUST

There is no month in the whole year, in which nature wears a more beautiful appearance than in the month of August. Spring has many beauties, and May is a fresh and blooming month, but the charms of this time of year are enhanced by their contrast with the winter season. August has no such advantage. It comes when we remember nothing but clear skies, green fields and sweet-smelling flowers—when the recollection of snow, and ice, and bleak winds, has faded from our minds as completely as they have disappeared from the earth,—and yet what a pleasant time it is! . . . A mellow softness appears to hang over the whole earth; the influence of the season seems to extend itself to the very waggon, whose slow motion across the well-reaped field, is perceptible only to the eye, but strikes with no harsh sound upon the ear.

The Pickwick Papers (1837)

AUGUST 1

OLIVER TWIST (1838)

Oh! the suspense, the fearful, acute suspense, of standing idly by while the life of one we dearly love, is trembling in the balance! Oh! the racking thoughts that crowd upon the mind, and make the heart beat violently, and the breath come thick, by the force of the images they conjure up before it; the desperate anxiety *to be doing something* to relieve the pain, or lessen the danger, which we have no power to alleviate; the sinking of soul and spirit, which the sad remembrance of our helplessness produces; what tortures can equal these; what reflections or endeavours can, in the full tide and fever of the time, allay them!

AUGUST 2

MARTIN CHUZZLEWIT (1844)

"I have draw'd upon A man, and fired upon A man for less," said Chollop, frowning. "I have know'd strong men obleeged to make themselves uncommon skase for less. I have know'd men Lynched for less, and beaten into punkin'-sarse for less, by an enlightened people. We are the intellect and virtue of the airth, the cream Of human natur', and the flower Of mortal force. Our backs is easy ris. We must be cracked-up, or they rises, and we snarls. We shows our teeth, I tell you, fierce. You'd better crack us up, you had!"

AUGUST 3

THE PICKWICK PAPERS (1837)

"There's nothin' so refreshin' as sleep, sir, as the servant-girl said afore she drank the egg-cupful o' laudanum" [said Sam Weller].

AUGUST 4

DOMBEY AND SON (1848)

The Doctor gently brushed the scattered ringlets of [Florence], aside from the face and mouth of the mother. Alas how calm they lay there; how little breath there was to stir them!

Thus, clinging fast to that slight spar within her arms, the mother drifted out upon the dark and unknown sea that rolls round all the world.

AUGUST 5

The members of this board were very sage, deep, philosophical men; and when they came to turn their attention to the workhouse, they found out at once, what ordinary folks would never have discovered—the poor people liked it! It was a regular place of public entertainment for the poorer classes; a tavern where there was nothing to pay; a public breakfast, dinner, tea, and supper all the year round; a brick and mortar elysium, where it was all play and no work. "Oho!" said the board, looking very knowing; "we are the fellows to set this to rights; we'll stop it all, in no time." So, they established the rule, that all poor people should have the alternative (for they would compel nobody, not they), of being starved by a gradual process in the house, or by a quick one out of it.

AUGUST 6

Wemmick explained to me while the Aged got his spectacles out, that this was according to custom, and that it gave the old gentleman infinite satisfaction to read the news aloud. "I won't offer an apology," said Wemmick, "for he isn't capable of many pleasures—are you, Aged P.?"

"All right, John, all right," returned the old man, seeing himself spoken to.

"Only tip him a nod every now and then when he looks off his paper," said Wemmick, "and he'll be happy as a king. We are all attention, Aged One."

AUGUST 7

"SEVEN DIALS—SCENES," SKETCHES BY BOZ (1836)

In addition to the numerous groups [in Seven Dials] who are idling about the gin-shops and squabbling in the centre of the road, every post in the open space has its occupant, who leans against it for hours, with listless perseverance. It is odd enough that one class of men in London appear to have no enjoyment beyond leaning against posts.

AUGUST 8

MARTIN CHUZZLEWIT (1844)

"Mrs. Gamp," [explained Mr. Mould,] "I'll tell you why it is [that people spend more on death than on birth]. It's because the laying out of money with a well-conducted establishment, where the thing is performed upon the very best scale, binds the broken heart, and sheds balm upon the wounded spirit. Hearts want binding, and spirits want balming when people die: not when people are born."

AUGUST 9

BLEAK HOUSE (1853)

Even these clerks were laughing. We glanced at the papers, and seeing Jarndyce and Jarndyce everywhere, asked an official-looking person who was standing in the midst of them, whether the cause was over. "Yes," he said; "it was all up with it at last!" and burst out laughing too.

AUGUST 10

GEORGE ORWELL ON DICKENS (1946)

The truth is that Dickens's criticism of society is almost exclusively moral. Hence the utter lack of any constructive suggestion anywhere in his work. He attacks the law, parliamentary government, the educational system and so forth, without ever clearly suggesting what he would put in their places. Of course it is not necessarily the business of a novelist, or a satirist, to make constructive suggestions, but the point is that Dickens's attitude is at bottom not even destructive. There is no clear sign that he wants the existing order to be overthrown, or that he believes it would make very much difference if it *were overthrown*. For in reality his target is not so much society as "human nature." It would be difficult to point anywhere in his books to a passage suggesting that the economic system is wrong *as a system*. Nowhere, for instance, does he make any attack on private enterprise or private property. Even in a book like *Our Mutual Friend*, which turns on the power of corpses to interfere with living people by means of idiotic wills, it does not occur to him to suggest that individuals ought not to have this irresponsible power. Of course one can draw this inference for oneself, and one can draw it again from the remarks about Bounderby's will at the end of *Hard Times*, and indeed from the whole of Dickens's work one can infer the evil of *laissez-faire* capitalism; but Dickens makes no such inference himself. It is said that Macaulay refused to review *Hard Times* because he disapproved of its "sullen Socialism." Obviously Macaulay is here using the word "Socialism" in the same sense in which, twenty years ago, a vegetarian meal or a Cubist picture used to be referred to as "Bolshevism." There is not a line in the book that can properly be called Socialistic; indeed, its tendency if anything is pro-capitalist, because its whole moral is that capitalists ought to be kind, not that workers ought to be rebellious. Bounderby is a bullying windbag and Gradgrind has been morally blinded, but if they were better men, the system would work well enough: that, all through, is the implication. And so far as social criticism goes, one can never extract much more from Dickens than this, unless one deliberately reads meanings into him. His whole "message" is one that at first glance looks like an enormous platitude: If men would behave decently the world would be decent.

AUGUST 11

HARD TIMES (1854)

It was very strange that a young gentleman who had never been left to his own guidance for five consecutive minutes, should be incapable at last of governing himself; but so it was with Tom [Gradgrind].

AUGUST 12

NICHOLAS NICKLEBY (1839)

"It only shows what Natur is, sir," said Mr. Squeers. "She's a rum 'un, is Natur."

AUGUST 13

THE OLD CURIOSITY SHOP (1841)

"I never saw any wax-work, ma'am," said Nell. "Is it funnier than Punch?"

"Funnier!" said Mrs. Jarley in a shrill voice. "It is not funny at all."

"Oh!" said Nell, with all possible humility.

"It isn't funny at all," repeated Mrs. Jarley. "It's calm and—what's that word again—critical?—no—classical, that's it—it is calm and classical. No low beatings and knockings about, no jokings and squeakings like your precious Punches, but always the same, with a constantly unchanging air of coldness and gentility; and so like life, that if wax-work only spoke and walked about, you'd hardly know the difference. I won't go so far as to say, that, as it is, I've seen wax-work quite like life, but I've certainly seen some life that was exactly like wax-work."

AUGUST 14

LITTLE DORRIT (1857)

"I want to know—" [started Arthur.]

"Look here. Upon my soul you mustn't come into the [Circumlocution Office] saying you want to know, you know," remonstrated Barnacle Junior, turning about and putting up the eye-glass.

AUGUST 15
OLIVER TWIST (1838)

There is a passion *for hunting something* deeply implanted in the human breast.

AUGUST 16
DAVID COPPERFIELD (1850)

"Ah!" he said, slowly turning his eyes towards me. "Well! If you was writin' to her, p'raps you'd recollect to say that Barkis was willin'; would you?"

"That Barkis was willing," I repeated, innocently. "Is that all the message?"

"Ye—es," he said, considering. "Ye—es. Barkis is willin.'"

AUGUST 17
BLEAK HOUSE (1853)

[Skimpole's] good friend Jarndyce and some other of his good friends then helped him . . . to several openings in life; but to no purpose, for he must confess to two of the oldest infirmities in the world: one was, that he had no idea of time; the other, that he had no idea of money. In consequence of which he never kept an appointment, never could transact any business, and never knew the value of anything! Well! So he had got on in life, and here he was!

AUGUST 18
GREAT EXPECTATIONS (1861)

In the little world in which children have their existence, whosoever brings them up, there is nothing so finely perceived and so finely felt, as injustice. It may be only small injustice that the child can be exposed to; but the child is small, and its world is small, and its rocking-horse stands as many hands high, according to scale, as a big-boned Irish hunter.

AUGUST 19
THE PICKWICK PAPERS (1837)

"Wot I like in that 'ere style of writin'," said the elder Mr. Weller, "is, that there ain't no callin' names in it,—no Wenuses, nor nothin' o' that kind. Wot's the good o' callin' a young 'ooman a Wenus or a angel, Sammy?"

"Ah! what, indeed?" replied Sam.

"You might jist as well call her a griffin, or a unicorn, or a king's arms at once, which is werry well known to be a col-lection o' fabulous animals," added Mr. Weller.

AUGUST 20

This [the United States] is not the Republic I came to see; this is not the Republic of my imagination. I infinitely prefer a liberal Monarchy—even with its sickening accompaniment of Court Circulars and Kings of Prussia—to such a Government as this. . . . The more I think of its youth and strength, the poorer and more trifling in a thousand respects it appears in my eyes.

AUGUST 21

The panic was so great [during the Gordon Riots] that the mails and stage-coaches were afraid to carry passengers who professed the obnoxious religion. If the drivers knew them, or they admitted that they held that creed, they would not take them, no, though they offered large sums; and yesterday, people had been afraid to recognize Catholic acquaintance in the streets, lest they should be marked by spies, and burnt out, as it was called, in consequence.

AUGUST 22

In the wildness of her sorrow, shame, and terror, the forlorn girl hurried through the sunshine of a bright morning, as if it were the darkness of a winter night. Wringing her hands and weeping bitterly, insensible to everything but the deep wound in her breast, stunned by the loss of all she loved, left like the sole survivor on a lonely shore from the wreck of a great vessel, [Florence] fled without a thought, without a hope, without a purpose, but to fly somewhere—anywhere.

AUGUST 23
OLIVER TWIST (1838)

"It's not Madness, ma'am," replied Mr. Bumble, after a few moments of deep meditation. "It's Meat."

AUGUST 24
MISS WADE'S "HISTORY OF A
SELF-TORMENTOR," LITTLE DORRIT (1857)

I have the misfortune of not being a fool. From a very early age I have detected what those about me thought they hid from me. If I could have been habitually imposed upon, instead of habitually discerning the truth, I might have lived as smoothly as most fools do.

AUGUST 25

DAVID COPPERFIELD (1850)

[Yarmouth] looked rather spongy and soppy, I thought, as I carried my eye over the great dull waste that lay across the river; and I could not help wondering, if the world were really as round as my geography-book said, how any part of it came to be so flat. But I reflected that Yarmouth might be situated at one of the poles; which would account for it.

AUGUST 26

MASTER HUMPHREY'S CLOCK (1840–41)

For who can wonder that man should feel a vague belief in tales of disembodied spirits wandering through those places which they once dearly affected, when he himself, scarcely less separated from his old world than they, is for ever lingering upon past emotions and bygone times, and hovering, the ghost of his former self, about the places and people that warmed his heart of old?

AUGUST 27

"Mind and matter," said the lady in the wig, "glide swift into the vortex of immensity. Howls the sublime, and softly sleeps the calm Ideal, in the whispering chambers of Imagination. To hear it, sweet it is. But then, outlaughs the stern philosopher, and saith to the Grotesque, 'What ho! arrest for me that Agency. Go, bring it here!' And so the vision fadeth."

AUGUST 28

"THE RUFFIAN,"
THE UNCOMMERCIAL TRAVELLER (1860)

It is to the saving up of the Ruffian class by the Magistracy and Police—to the conventional preserving of them, as if they were Partridges—that their number and audacity must be in great part referred. Why is a notorious Thief and Ruffian ever left at large? He never turns his liberty to any account but violence and plunder, he never did a day's work out of gaol, he never will do a day's work out of gaol.

AUGUST 29

Within the altar of the old village church there stands a white marble tablet, which bears as yet but one word: "AGNES." There is no coffin in that tomb; and may it be many, many years, before another name is placed above it! But, if the spirits of the Dead ever come back to earth, to visit spots hallowed by the love—the love beyond the grave—of those whom they knew in life, I believe that the shade of Agnes sometimes hovers round that solemn nook. I believe it none the less because that nook is in a Church, and she was weak and erring.

AUGUST 30

"No Popery, brother!" cried the hangman.

"No Property, brother!" responded Hugh.

"Popery, Popery," said the secretary with his usual mildness.

"It's all the same!" cried Dennis. "It's all right. Down with him, Muster Gashford. Down with everybody, down with everything! Hurrah for the Protestant religion! That's the time of day, Muster Gashford!"

"[Nell's] so," said Quilp, speaking very slowly, and feigning to be quite absorbed in the subject, "so small, so compact, so beautifully modelled, so fair, with such blue veins and such a transparent skin, and such little feet, and such winning ways—but, bless me, you're nervous [Grandfather]! Why, neighbour, what's the matter? I swear to you . . . that I had no idea old blood ran so fast or kept so warm. I thought it was sluggish in its course, and cool, quite cool. I am pretty sure it ought to be. Yours must be out of order, neighbour."

SEPTEMBER

Being in a humour for complete solitude and unin-
terrupted meditation this autumn, I have taken a
lodging for six weeks in the most unfrequented part
of England—in a word, in London.

"Arcadian London,"
The Uncommercial Traveller (1860)

SEPTEMBER 1

"Stop thief! Stop thief!" The cry is taken up by a hundred voices, and the crowd accumulate at every turning. Away they fly, splashing through the mud, and rattling along the pavements: up go the windows, out run the people, onward bear the mob, a whole audience desert Punch in the very thickest of the plot, and, joining the rushing throng, swell the shout, and lend fresh vigour to the cry, "Stop thief! Stop thief!"

. . . One wretched breathless child, panting with exhaustion; terror in his looks; agony in his eyes; large drops of perspiration streaming down his face; strains every nerve to make head upon his pursuers; and as they follow on his track, and gain upon him every instant, they hail his decreasing strength with still louder shouts, and whoop and scream with joy. "Stop thief!" Ay, stop him for God's sake, were it only in mercy!

SEPTEMBER 2

"And as to husbands," [said Mrs. Gamp,] "there's a wooden leg gone likewise home to its account, which in its constancy of walkin' into wine vaults, and never comin' out again 'till fetched by force, was quite as weak as flesh, if not weaker."

SEPTEMBER 3
GREAT EXPECTATIONS (1861)

It is a most miserable thing to feel ashamed of home. There may be black ingratitude in the thing, and the punishment may be retributive and well deserved; but, that it *is* a miserable thing, I can testify.

Home had never been a very pleasant place to me, because of my sister's temper. But, Joe had sanctified it, and I believed in it.

SEPTEMBER 4
"A LITTLE DINNER IN AN HOUR," THE UNCOMMERCIAL TRAVELLER (1860)

I hold phrenology, within certain limits, to be true; I am much of the same mind as to the subtler expressions of the hand; I hold physiognomy to be infallible; though all these sciences demand rare qualities in the student.

SEPTEMBER 5
DAVID COPPERFIELD (1850)

I look at the sunlight coming in at the open door through the porch, and there I see a stray sheep—I don't mean a sinner, but mutton—half making up his mind to come into the church. I feel that if I looked at him any longer, I might be tempted to say something out loud; and what would become of me then! I look up at the monumental tablets on the wall, and try to think of Mr. Bodgers late of this parish, and what the feelings of Mrs. Bodgers must have been, when afflictions sore, long time Mr. Bodgers bore, and physicians were in vain. I wonder whether they called in Mr. Chillip, and he was in vain; and, if so, how he likes to be reminded of it once a week.

SEPTEMBER 6

A TALE OF TWO CITIES (1859)

A wonderful fact to reflect upon, that every human creature is constituted to be that profound secret and mystery to every other.

SEPTEMBER 7

DOMBEY AND SON (1848)

[T]hen he heard the loud clock in the hall still gravely inquiring "how, is, my, lit, tle, friend? how, is, my, lit, tle, friend?" as it had done before.

He sat, with folded hands, upon his pedestal, silently listening. But he might have answered "weary, weary! very lonely, very sad!" And there, with an aching void in his young heart, and all outside so cold, and bare, and strange, Paul sat as if he had taken life unfurnished, and the upholsterers were never coming.

SEPTEMBER 8

MASTER HUMPHREY'S CLOCK (1840–41)

There are some few people well to do, who remember to have heard it said, that numbers of men and women—thousands, they think it was—get up in London every day, unknowing where to lay their heads at night; and that there are quarters of the town where misery and famine always are. They don't quite believe it,— there may be some truth in it, but it is exaggerated, of course. So, each of these thousand worlds goes on, intent upon itself, until night comes again,—first with its lights and pleasures, and its cheerful streets; then with its guilt and darkness.

SEPTEMBER 9

THE PICKWICK PAPERS (1837)

My dear Sammle,

I am wery sorry to have the pleasure of bein a Bear of ill news your Mother in law cort cold consekens of imprudently settin too long on the damp grass in the rain. . . . [H]er veels wos immedetly greased and everythink done to set her agoin as could be inwented your father had hopes as she vould have vorked round as usual but just as she wos a turnen the corner my boy she took the wrong road and vent down hill vith a welocity you never see and notvithstanding that the drag wos put on drectly by the medikel man it wornt of no use at all for she paid the last pike at twenty minutes afore six o'clock yesterday evenin having done the journey wery much under the reglar time vich praps was partly owen to her haven taken in wery little luggage.

SEPTEMBER 10

"AN OLD STAGE-COACHING HOUSE," THE
UNCOMMERCIAL TRAVELLER (1860)

Before the waitress had shut the door, I had forgotten how many stage-coaches she said used to change horses in the town every day. But it was of little moment; any high number would do as well as another. It had been a great stage-coaching town in the great stage-coaching times, and the ruthless railways had killed and buried it.

SEPTEMBER 11

BLEAK HOUSE (1853)

Name, Jo. Nothing else that he knows on. Don't know that everybody has two names. Never heerd of sich a think. Don't know that Jo is short for a longer name. Thinks it long enough for *him*. *He* don't find no fault with it. Spell it? No. *He* can't spell it. No father, no mother, no friends. Never been to school. What's home?

SEPTEMBER 12

LITTLE DORRIT (1857)

Mr. Tite Barnacle was a buttoned-up man, and consequently a weighty one. All buttoned-up men are weighty. All buttoned-up men are believed in. Whether or no the reserved and never-exercised power of unbuttoning, fascinates mankind; whether or no wisdom is supposed to condense and augment when buttoned up, and to evaporate when unbuttoned; it is certain that the man to whom importance is accorded is the buttoned-up man.

SEPTEMBER 13

PICTURES FROM ITALY (1846)

And let us not remember Italy the less regardfully, because, in every fragment of her fallen Temples, and every stone of her deserted palaces and prisons, she helps to inculcate the lesson that the wheel of Time is rolling for an end, and that the world is, in all great essentials, better, gentler, more forbearing, and more hopeful, as it rolls!

SEPTEMBER 14

"ASTLEY'S—SCENES," SKETCHES BY BOZ (1836)

We defy any one who has been to Astley's two or three times, and is consequently capable of appreciating the perseverance with which precisely the same jokes are repeated night after night, and season after season, not to be amused ... [by] the scenes in the circle. For ourself, we know that when the hoop, composed of jets of gas, is let down ... we feel as much enlivened as the youngest child present.

What! shall we declaim against the ignorant peasantry of Ireland, and mince the matter when these American task-masters are in question? Shall we cry shame on the brutality of those who ham-string cattle: and spare the lights of Freedom upon earth who notch the ears of men and women, cut pleasant posies in the shrinking flesh, learn to write with pens of red-hot iron on the human face, rack their poetic fancies for liveries of mutilation which their slaves shall wear for life and carry to the grave, breaking living limbs as did the soldiery who mocked and slew the Saviour of the world, and set defenceless creatures up for targets!

SEPTEMBER 16

THE PICKWICK PAPERS (1837)

"Now, attend, Mr. Weller," said Serjeant Buzfuz, dipping a large pen into the inkstand before him, for the purpose of frightening Sam with the show of taking down his answer. "You were in the passage, and yet saw nothing of what was going forward. Have you a pair of eyes, Mr. Weller?"

"Yes, I have a pair of eyes," replied Sam, "and that's just it. If they wos a pair 'o patent double million magnifyin' gas microscopes of hextra power, p'raps I might be able to see through a flight o' stairs and a deal door; but bein' only eyes, you see, my wision's limited."

SEPTEMBER 17

MARTIN CHUZZLEWIT (1844)

"And eggs," said Mr. Pecksniff, "even they have their moral. See how they come and go! Every pleasure is transitory. We can't even eat, long. If we indulge in harmless fluids, we get the dropsy; if in exciting liquids, we get drunk. What a soothing reflection is that!"

"Don't say *we* get drunk, Pa," urged the eldest Miss Pecksniff.

"When I say we, my dear," returned her father, "I mean mankind in general; the human race, considered as a body, and not as individuals. There is nothing personal in morality, my love."

SEPTEMBER 18

THE PICKWICK PAPERS (1837)

"Vell," said Mr. Weller, "now I s'pose he'll want to call some witnesses to speak to his character, or p'raps to prove a alleybi. I've been a turnin' the bis'ness over in my mind, and he may make his-self easy, Sammy. I've got some friends as'll do either for him, but my adwice 'ud be this here—never mind the character, and stick to the alleybi. Nothing like a alleybi, Sammy, nothing." . . . .

"I know'd what 'ud come o' this here mode o' doin' bisness. Oh Sammy, Sammy, vy worn't there a alleybi!"

SEPTEMBER 19

THE OLD CURIOSITY SHOP (1841)

When they came to any town or village, or even to a detached house of good appearance, Short blew a blast upon the brazen trumpet and carolled a fragment of a song in that hilarious tone common to Punches and their consorts. If people hurried to the windows, Mr. Codlin pitched the temple, and hastily unfurling the drapery and concealing Short therewith, flourished hysterically on the pipes and performed an air. Then the entertainment began as soon as might be; Mr. Codlin having the responsibility of deciding on its length and of protracting or expediting the time for the hero's final triumph over the enemy of mankind, according as he judged that the after-crop of halfpence would be plentiful or scant. When it had been gathered in to the last farthing, he resumed his load and on they went again.

SEPTEMBER 20

LITTLE DORRIT (1857)

[Arthur and Amy] went quietly down into the roaring streets, inseparable and blessed; and as they passed along in sunshine and shade, the noisy and the eager, and the arrogant and the froward and the vain, fretted, and chafed, and made their usual uproar.

SEPTEMBER 21

GRAHAM GREENE ON DICKENS (1951)

Is it too fantastic to imagine that in this novel [*Oliver Twist*], as in many of his later books, creeps in, unrecognized by the author, the eternal and alluring taint of the Manichee, with its simple and terrible explanation of our plight, how the world was made by Satan and not by God, lulling us with the music of despair?

SEPTEMBER 22

"MUGBY JUNCTION," CHRISTMAS STORIES (1866)

I am the boy at Mugby. That's about what *I* am.

You don't know what I mean? What a pity! But I think you do. I think you must. Look here. I am the boy at what is called The Refreshment Room at

Mugby Junction, and what's proudest boast is, that it never yet refreshed a mortal being.

SEPTEMBER 23

THE MYSTERY OF EDWIN DROOD (1870)

The host had gone below to the cellar, and had brought up bottles of ruby, straw-coloured, and golden drinks, which had ripened long ago in lands where no fogs are, and had since lain slumbering in the shade. Sparkling and tingling after so long a nap, they pushed at their corks to help the corkscrew (like prisoners helping rioters to force their gates), and danced out gaily.

SEPTEMBER 24

DAVID COPPERFIELD (1850)

Mr. Barkis poked [his stick] against a box. . . .

"Old clothes," said Mr. Barkis.

"Oh!" said I.

"I wish it was Money, sir," said Mr. Barkis.

"I wish it was, indeed," said I.

"But it AIN'T," said Mr. Barkis, opening both his eyes as wide as he possibly could.

SEPTEMBER 25

"And so the poor creatur's dead! I'm sorry for it. She warn't a bad-disposed 'ooman, if them shepherds had let her alone. I'm wery sorry for it."

Mr. [Sam] Weller uttered those words in so serious a manner, that the pretty housemaid cast down her eyes and looked very grave.

"Hows'ever . . . it wos to be—and wos, as the old lady said arter she'd married the footman. Can't be helped now, can it, Mary?"

SEPTEMBER 26

[The Pecksniff sisters were] not ecstatically charmed to be awakened . . . by certain dulcet strains breaking in upon the silent watches of the night.

It was very affecting, very. Nothing more dismal could have been desired by the most fastidious taste. The gentleman of a vocal turn was head mute, or chief mourner; Jinkins took the bass; and the rest took anything they could get. The youngest gentleman blew his melancholy into a flute. He didn't blow much out of it, but that was all the better. If the two Miss Pecksniffs and Mrs. Todgers had perished by spontaneous combustion, and the serenade had been in honour of their ashes, it would have been impossible to surpass the unutterable despair expressed in that one chorus, "Go where glory waits thee!" It was a requiem, a dirge, a moan, a howl, a wail, a lament, an abstract of everything that is sorrowful and hideous in sound.

SEPTEMBER 27

A TALE OF TWO CITIES (1859)

A bottle of good claret after dinner does a digger in the red coals no harm, otherwise than as it has a tendency to throw him out of work.

SEPTEMBER 28

OUR MUTUAL FRIEND (1865)

"[I] merely referred," Mr. Podsnap explained, with a sense of meritorious proprietorship, "to our Constitution, Sir. We Englishmen are Very Proud of our Constitution, Sir. It Was Bestowed Upon Us By Providence. No Other Country is so Favoured as This Country."

"And ozer countries?—" the foreign gentleman was beginning, when Mr. Podsnap put him right again.

"We do not say Ozer; we say Other: the letters are 'T' and 'H;' you say Tay and Aish, You Know;" (still with clemency). "The sound is 'th'—'th'!"

"And *other* countries," said the foreign gentleman. "They do how?"

"They do, Sir," returned Mr. Podsnap, gravely shaking his head; "they do—I am sorry to be obliged to say it—*as* they do."

"Good day, sir!"

"What?" said he.

"Good day, sir."

He seemed to consider about that, and not to agree with me.—"Was you a looking for anything?" he then asked, in a pointed manner.

"I was wondering whether there happened to be any fragment of an old stage-coach here."

"Is that all?"

"That's all."

"No, there ain't."

I whistled and made nothing of going. But the village was very peaceful and quiet, and the light mists were solemnly rising, as if to show me the world, and I had been so innocent and little there, and all beyond was so unknown and great, that in a moment with a strong heave and sob I broke into tears. It was by the finger-post at the end of the village, and I laid my hand upon it, and said, "Good-bye, O my dear, dear friend!"

OCTOBER

It happened to be an iron-grey autumnal day, with a shrewd east wind blowing—a day in keeping with the proceedings. Mr. Dombey represented in himself the wind, the shade, and the autumn of the christening. He stood in his library to receive the company, as hard and cold as the weather; and when he looked out through the glass room, at the trees in the little garden, their brown and yellow leaves came fluttering down, as if he blighted them.

Dombey and Son (1848)

OCTOBER 1

"I have reason to know, sir," interrupted the colonel, "that the aristocratic circles of your country quail before the name of Jefferson Brick. I should like to be informed, sir, from your lips, which of his sentiments has struck the deadliest blow—"

"At the hundred heads of the Hydra of Corruption now grovelling in the dust beneath the lance of Reason, and spouting up to the universal arch above us, its sanguinary gore," said Mr. Brick, putting on a little blue cloth cap with a glazed front, and quoting his last article.

OCTOBER 2

"I've been done everything to, pretty well—except hanged" [said Magwitch]. "I've been locked up, as much as a silver tea-kittle. I've been carted here and carted there, and put out of this town and put out of that town, and stuck in the stocks, and whipped and worried and drove. I've no more notion where I was born than you have—if so much. I first become aware of myself, down in Essex, a thieving turnips for my living. Summun had run away from me—a man—a tinker—and he'd took the fire with him, and left me wery cold."

OCTOBER 3

BARNABY RUDGE (1841)

Now, now, the door was down. Now [the Gordon riot-ers] came rushing through the jail, calling to each other in the vaulted passages; clashing the iron gates dividing yard from yard; beating at the doors of cells and wards; wrenching off bolts and locks and bars; tearing down the door-posts to get men out; endeav-ouring to drag them by main force through gaps and windows where a child could scarcely pass; whoop-ing and yelling without a moment's rest; and run-ning through the heat and flames as if they were cased in metal.

OCTOBER 4

OLIVER TWIST (1838)

"The board allow you coals, don't they, Mrs. Cor-ney?" inquired the beadle, affectionately pressing her hand.

"And candles," replied Mrs. Corney, slightly re-turning the pressure.

"Coals, candles, and house-rent free," said Mr. Bumble. "Oh, Mrs. Corney, what a Angel you are!"

The lady was not proof against this burst of feel-ing. She sank into Mr. Bumble's arms; and that gen-tleman in his agitation, imprinted a passionate kiss upon her chaste nose.

"Such porochial perfection!" exclaimed Mr. Bumble, rapturously.

OCTOBER 5

BLEAK HOUSE (1853)

Why, Mrs. Piper has a good deal to say, chiefly in parentheses and without punctuation, but not much to tell. Mrs. Piper lives in the court (which her husband is a cabinet-maker), and it has long been well beknown among the neighbours (counting from the day next but one before the half-baptising of Alexander James Piper aged eighteen months and four days old on accounts of not being expected to live such was the sufferings gentlemen of that child in his gums) as the Plaintive—so Mrs. Piper insists on calling the deceased—was reported to have sold himself. Thinks it was the Plaintive's air in which that report originatinin. See the Plaintive often and considered as his air was feariocious and not to be allowed to go about some children being timid.

OCTOBER 6

MARTIN CHUZZLEWIT (1844)

[F]estive preparations on a rather extensive scale were already completed, and the two Miss Pecksniffs were awaiting their return with hospitable looks. There were two bottles of currant wine, white and red; a dish of sandwiches (very long and very slim); another of apples; another of captain's biscuits (which are always a moist and jovial sort of viand); a plate of oranges cut up small and gritty; with powdered sugar, and a highly geological home-made cake.

OCTOBER 7

NICHOLAS NICKLEBY (1839)

"Just lift that little boy off the tall stool in the back office, and tell him to come in here, will you, my man?" said Squeers. . . . "Oh, he's lifted his-self off! My son, sir, little Wackford. What do you think of him, sir, for a specimen of the Dotheboys Hall feeding? Ain't he fit to bust out of his clothes, and start the seams, and make the very buttons fly off with his fatness? Here's flesh!" cried Squeers, turning the boy about, and indenting the plumpest parts of his figure with diverse pokes and punches, to the great discomposure of his son and heir. "Here's firmness, here's solidness!"

OCTOBER 8

Mr. Pickwick wandered along all the [prison] galleries, up and down all the staircases, and once again round the whole area of the yard. The great body of the prison population appeared to be Mivins, and Smangle, and the parson, and the butcher, and the leg, over and over, and over again. . . . The whole place seemed restless and troubled; and the people were crowding and flitting to and fro, like the shadows in an uneasy dream.

"I have seen enough," said Mr. Pickwick, as he threw himself into a chair in his little apartment. "My head aches with these scenes, and my heart too. Henceforth I will be a prisoner in my own room."

OCTOBER 9

This may be fancy, though I think the memory of most of us can go farther back into [childhood and infancy] than many of us suppose; just as I believe the power of observation in numbers of very young children to be quite wonderful for its closeness and accuracy. Indeed, I think that most grown men who are remarkable in this respect, may with greater propriety be said not to have lost the faculty, than to have acquired it.

OCTOBER 10

THE OLD CURIOSITY SHOP (1841)

"May the present moment," said Dick [Swiveller], sticking his fork into a large carbuncular potato, "be the worst of our lives! I like this plan of sending 'em with the peel on; there's a charm in drawing a potato from its native element (if I may so express it) to which the rich and powerful are strangers. Ah! 'Man wants but little here below, nor wants that little long!' How true that is!—after dinner."

OCTOBER 11

"PRIVATE THEATRES—SCENES,"
SKETCHES BY BOZ (1836)

"RICHARD THE THIRD.—DUKE OF GLO'STER, 2*l*.; EARL OF RICHMOND, 1*l*.; DUKE OF BUCKINGHAM, 15*s*.; CATESBY, 12*s*.; TRESSEL, 10*s*. 6*d*.; LORD STANLEY, 5*s*.; LORD MAYOR OF LONDON, 2*s*. 6*d*."

Such are the written placards wafered up in the gentlemen's dressing-room . . . at a private theatre; and such are the sums extracted from the shop-till, or overcharged in the office expenditure, by the donkeys who are prevailed upon to pay for permission to exhibit their lamentable ignorance and boobyism on the stage of a private theatre.

OCTOBER 12

Some philosophers tell us that selfishness is at the root of our best loves and affections. Mr. Dombey's young child was, from the beginning, so distinctly important to him as a part of his own greatness, or (which is the same thing) of the greatness of Dombey and Son, that there is no doubt his parental affection might have been easily traced . . . to a very low foundation. But he loved his son with all the love he had.

OCTOBER 13

"BILL-STICKING," THE UNCOMMERCIAL
TRAVELLER (1860)

If I had an enemy whom I hated—which Heaven forbid!—and if I knew of something which sat heavy on his conscience, I think I would introduce that something into a Posting-Bill, and place a large impression in the hands of an active sticker. I can scarcely imagine a more terrible revenge. I should haunt him, by this means, night and day.

OCTOBER 14

"[T]he world has gone past me [said Sol Gillis]. I don't blame it; but I no longer understand it. Tradesmen are not the same as they used to be, apprentices are not the same, business is not the same, business commodities are not the same. Seven-eighths of my stock is old-fashioned. I am an old-fashioned man in an old-fashioned shop, in a street that is not the same as I remember it. I have fallen behind the time, and am too old to catch it again. Even the noise it makes a long way ahead, confuses me."

OCTOBER 15

"Hold there, you and your philanthropy," cried the smiling landlady. . . . "I know nothing of philosophical philanthropy. But I know what I have seen. . . . And I tell you this, my friend, that there are people . . . who have no good in them—none. That there are people whom it is necessary to detest without compromise. That there are people who must be dealt with as enemies of the human race. That there are people who have no human heart, and who must be crushed like savage beasts and cleared out of the way."

OCTOBER 16

[The play was in progress, but I had to tell her I was here.] "Agnes!" I said, thickly, "Lorblessmer! Agnes!"

"Hush! Pray!" she answered, I could not conceive why. "You disturb the company. Look at the stage!"

I tried, on her injunction, to fix it, and to hear something of what was going on there, but quite in vain. I looked at her again by-and-bye, and saw her shrink into her corner, and put her gloved hand to her forehead.

"Agnes!" I said. "I'mafraidyou'renorwell."

OCTOBER 17

"The word politics, sir," said Mr. Pickwick, "comprises, in itself, a difficult study of no inconsiderable magnitude."

"Ah!" said the Count, drawing out the tablets again, "ver good—fine words to begin a chapter. Chapter forty-seven. Poltics. The word poltic surprises by himself—" And down went Mr. Pickwick's remark, in Count Smorltork's tablets, with such variations and additions as the count's exuberant fancy suggested, or his imperfect knowledge of the language, occasioned.

OCTOBER 18

"A porochial life, ma'am," continued Mr. Bumble, striking the table with his cane, "is a life of worrit, and vexation, and hardihood; but all public characters, as I may say, must suffer prosecution."

OCTOBER 19

"NIGHT WALKS," THE UNCOMMERCIAL
TRAVELLER (1860)

Covent-garden Market, when it was market morning, was wonderful company. The great waggons of cabbages, with growers' men and boys lying asleep under them, and with sharp dogs from market-garden neighbourhoods looking after the whole, were as good as a party.

OCTOBER 20

"THE LONG VOYAGE," REPRINTED PIECES (1868)

When the wind is blowing and the sleet or rain is driving against the dark windows, I love to sit by the fire, thinking of what I have read in books of voyage and travel. Such books have had a strong fascination for my mind from my earliest childhood; and

I wonder it should have come to pass that I never have been round the world, never have been ship-wrecked, ice-environed, tomahawked, or eaten.

OCTOBER 21

OUR MUTUAL FRIEND (1865)

Errands gone
On with fi
Delity By
Ladies and Gentlemen
I remain
Your humble Servt.
Silas Wegg.

OCTOBER 22

"THE BATTLE OF LIFE," CHRISTMAS BOOKS (1846)

Snitchey and Craggs had a snug little office on the old Battle Ground, where they drove a snug little business, and fought a great many small pitched battles for a great many contending parties. Though it could hardly be said of these conflicts that they were running fights—for in truth they generally proceeded at a snail's pace—the part the Firm had in them came so far within the general denomination, that now they took a shot at this Plaintiff, and now aimed a chop at that Defendant, now made a heavy charge at an estate in Chancery, and now had some light skirmishing among an irregular body of small debtors, just as the occasion served, and the enemy happened to present himself.

OCTOBER 23
DAVID COPPERFIELD (1850)

As soon as I could creep away, I crept up-stairs. My old dear bedroom was changed, and I was to lie a long way off. I rambled down-stairs to find anything that was like itself, so altered it all seemed; and roamed into the yard. I very soon started back from there, for the empty dog-kennel was filled up with a great dog—deep-mouthed and black-haired like [Mr. Murdstone]—and he was very angry at the sight of me, and sprang out to get at me.

OCTOBER 24
BLEAK HOUSE (1853)

Do you hear, Jo? It is nothing to you or to any one else, that the great lights of the parliamentary sky have failed for some few years, in this business, to set you the example of moving on. The one grand recipe remains for you—the profound philosophical prescription—the be-all and the end-all of your strange existence upon earth. Move on! You are by no means to move off, Jo, for the great lights can't at all agree about that. Move on!

OCTOBER 25

LITTLE DORRIT (1857)

Flora, always tall, had grown to be very broad too, and short of breath; but that was not much. Flora, whom he had left a lily, had become a peony; but that was not much. Flora, who had seemed enchanting in all she said and thought, was diffuse and silly. That was much. Flora, who had been spoiled and artless long ago, was determined to be spoiled and artless now. That was a fatal blow.

OCTOBER 26

GREAT EXPECTATIONS (1861)

Once for all; I knew to my sorrow, often and often, if not always, that I loved her against reason, against promise, against peace, against hope, against happiness, against all discouragement that could be.

OCTOBER 27

GREAT EXPECTATIONS (1861)

I took [Estella's] hand in mine, and we went out of the ruined place; and, as the morning mists had risen long ago when I first left the forge, so, the evening mists were rising now, and in all the broad expanse of tranquil light they showed to me, I saw no shadow of another parting from her.

OCTOBER 28

A TALE OF TWO CITIES (1859)

[Newgate] was a vile place, in which most kinds of debauchery and villainy were practised, and where dire diseases were bred, that came into court with the prisoners, and sometimes rushed straight from the dock at my Lord Chief Justice himself, and pulled him off the bench.

OCTOBER 29

HARD TIMES (1854)

"Ladies and gentlemen, I am Josiah Bounderby of Coketown. Since you have done my wife and myself the honour of drinking our healths and happiness, I suppose I must acknowledge the same; though, as you all know me, and know what I am, and what my extraction was, you won't expect a speech from a man who, when he sees a Post, says 'that's a Post,' and when he sees a Pump, says 'that's a Pump,' and is not to be got to call a Post a Pump, or a Pump a Post, or either of them a Toothpick."

OCTOBER 30

"EARLY COACHES—SCENES,"
SKETCHES BY BOZ (1836)

We have often wondered how many months' incessant travelling in a post-chaise it would take to kill a man; and wondering by analogy, we should very much like to know how many months of constant travelling in a succession of early coaches, an unfortunate mortal could endure. Breaking a man alive upon the wheel, would be nothing to breaking his rest, his peace, his heart—everything but his fast.

+

BILST

UM

PSHI

S.M.

ARK

NOVEMBER

London. Michaelmas Term lately over, and the Lord
Chancellor sitting in Lincoln's Inn Hall. Implacable
November weather. As much mud in the streets, as
if the waters had but newly retired from the face of
the earth, and it would not be wonderful to meet a
Megalosaurus, forty feet long or so, waddling like an
elephantine lizard up Holborn Hill.

Bleak House (1853)

NOVEMBER 1

The funeral of the deceased lady having been "performed" to the entire satisfaction of the undertaker, as well as of the neighbourhood at large . . . , the various members of Mr. Dombey's household subsided into their several places in the domestic system. . . . [W]hen the cook had said she was a quiet-tempered lady, and the house-keeper had said it was the common lot, and the butler had said who'd have thought it, and the housemaid had said she couldn't hardly believe it, and the footman had said it seemed exactly like a dream, they had quite worn the subject out, and began to think their mourning was wearing rusty too.

NOVEMBER 2

HARD TIMES (1854)

Mrs. Sparsit . . . kept such a sharp look-out, night and day, under her Coriolanian eyebrows, that her eyes, like a couple of lighthouses on an iron-bound coast, might have warned all prudent mariners from that bold rock her Roman nose and the dark and craggy region in its neighborhood.

"Why, truly, sir," Mr. Wegg admitted with modesty; "I believe you couldn't show me the piece of English print, that I wouldn't be equal to collaring and throwing."

"On the spot?" said Mr. Boffin.

"On the spot."

"I know'd it! Then consider this. Here am I, a man without a wooden leg, and yet all print is shut to me."

"Indeed, sir?" Mr. Wegg returned with increasing self-complacency. "Education neglected?"

"Neg—lected!" repeated Boffin, with emphasis. "That ain't no word for it. I don't mean to say but what if you showed me a B, I could so far give you change for it, as to answer Boffin."

"Come, come, sir," said Mr. Wegg, throwing in a little encouragement, "that's something, too."

"It's something," answered Mr. Boffin, "but I'll take my oath it ain't much."

NOVEMBER 4

LETTER TO ANGELA BURDETT-COUTTS
(MAY 11, 1855)

The people will not bear for any length of time what they bear now. I see it clearly written in every truthful indication that I am capable of discerning everywhere. And I want to interpose something between them and their wrath.

For this reason solely, I am a Reformer heart and soul. . . . I am in desperate earnest, because I know it is a desperate case.

NOVEMBER 5

DAVID COPPERFIELD (1850)

I began one note [of apology to Agnes], in a six-syllable line, "Oh, do not remember"—but that associated itself with the fifth of November, and became an absurdity.

NOVEMBER 6

JOHN RUSKIN ON DICKENS (1860)

The essential value and truth of Dickens's writings have been unwisely lost sight of by many thoughtful persons, merely because he presents his truth with some colour of caricature. . . . But let us not lose the use of Dickens's wit and insight, because he chooses to speak in a circle of stage fire. He is entirely right in his main drift and purpose in every book he has written; and all of them . . . should be studied with close and earnest care by persons interested in social questions.

"Oh you little villain!" said [Mrs. Todgers]. "Oh you bad, false boy!"

"No worse than yerself," retorted Bailey, guarding his head, on a principle invented by Mr. Thomas Cribb. "Ah! Come now! Do that again, will yer?"

"He's the most dreadful child," said Mrs. Todgers, setting down the dish, "I ever had to deal with. The gentlemen spoil him to that extent, and teach him such things, that I'm afraid nothing but hanging will ever do him any good."

"Won't it!" cried Bailey. "Oh! Yes! Wot do you go a-lowerin the table-beer for then, and destroying my constitooshun?"

We understand Dickens in Russia, I am convinced, almost as well as the English, and maybe even all the subtleties; maybe even we love him no less than his own countrymen; and yet how typical, distinctive, and national Dickens is.

NOVEMBER 9

BLEAK HOUSE (1853)

That one cold winter night, when [Jo] was shivering in a doorway near his crossing, the man turned to look at him, and came back, and, having questioned him and found that he had not a friend in the world, said, "Neither have I. Not one!" and gave him the price of a supper and a night's lodging. That the man had often spoken to him since; and asked him whether he slept sound at night, and how he bore cold and hunger, and whether he ever wished to die; and similar strange questions. That when the man had no money, he would say in passing, "I am as poor as you to-day, Jo;" but when he had any, he had always . . . been glad to give him some.

"He wos wery good to me," says the boy, wiping his eyes with his wretched sleeve. "Wen I see him a-layin' so stritched out just now, I wished he could have heerd me tell him so. He wos wery good to me, he wos!"

NOVEMBER 10

THE PICKWICK PAPERS (1837)

"You think so now," said Mr. Weller, with the gravity of age, "but you'll find that as you get vider, you'll get viser. Vidth and visdom, Sammy, alvays grows together."

NOVEMBER 11

The couple who dote upon their children have usually a great many of them: six or eight at least. The children are either the healthiest in all the world, or the most unfortunate in existence. In either case, they are equally the theme of their doting parents, and equally a source of mental anguish and irritation to their doting parents' friends.

NOVEMBER 12

DAVID COPPERFIELD (1850)

"Barkis, my dear!" said Peggotty.

"C. P. Barkis," he cried faintly. "No better woman anywhere!"

"Look! Here's Master Davy!" said Peggotty. For he now opened his eyes.

I was on the point of asking him if he knew me, when he tried to stretch out his arm, and said to me, distinctly, with a pleasant smile:

"Barkis is willin'!"

And, it being low water, he went out with the tide.

"Flora. I assure you, Flora, I am happy in seeing you once more, and in finding that, like me, you have not forgotten the old foolish dreams, when we saw all before us in the light of our youth and hope."

"You don't seem so," pouted Flora, "you take it very coolly, but however I know you are disappointed in me, I suppose the Chinese ladies—Mandarinesses if you call them so—are the cause or perhaps I am the cause myself, it's just as likely."

"No, no," Clennam entreated, "don't say that."

"Oh I must you know," said Flora, in a positive tone, "what nonsense not to, I know I am not what you expected, I know that very well."

NOVEMBER 14

AMERICAN NOTES (1842)

No amusements? . . . What are the fifty newspapers, which those precocious urchins are bawling down the street, and which are kept filled within, what are they but amusements? Not vapid waterish amusements, but good strong stuff; dealing in round abuse and blackguard names; pulling off the roofs of private houses . . . pimping and pandering for all degrees of vicious taste, and gorging with coined lies the most voracious maw.

NOVEMBER 15

BARNABY RUDGE (1841)

To be shelterless and alone in the open country, hearing the wind moan and watching for day through the whole long weary night; to listen to the falling rain, and crouch for warmth beneath the lee of some old barn or rick, or in the hollow of a tree; are dismal things—but not so dismal as the wandering up and down where shelter is, and beds and sleepers are by thousands; a houseless rejected creature.

NOVEMBER 16

DAVID COPPERFIELD (1850)

"No, Miss Mowcher," I replied. "Her name is Emily."

"Aha?" she cried. . . . "Umph? What a rattle I am! Mr. Copperfield, ain't I volatile?"

NOVEMBER 17

"PREFACE" TO NICHOLAS NICKLEBY (1839)

The Author's object in calling public attention to the system [of the Yorkshire schools] would be very imperfectly fulfilled, if he did not state now, in his own person, emphatically and earnestly, that Mr. Squeers and his school are faint and feeble pictures of an existing reality, purposely subdued and kept down lest they should be deemed impossible. That there are, upon record, trials at law in which damages have been sought as a poor recompense for lasting agonies and disfigurements inflicted upon children by the treatment of the master in these places, involving such offensive and foul details of neglect, cruelty, and disease, as no writer of fiction would have the boldness to imagine. And that, since he has been engaged upon these Adventures, he has received, from private quarters far beyond the reach of suspicion or distrust, accounts of atrocities, in the perpetuation of which upon neglected or repudiated children, these schools have been the main instruments, very far exceeding any that appear in these pages.

NOVEMBER 18

"OUR BORE," REPRINTED PIECES (1868)

At one period in his life, our bore had an illness. It was an illness of a dangerous character for society at large. Innocently remark that you are very well, or that somebody else is very well; and our bore, with a preface that one never knows what a blessing health is until one has lost it, is reminded of that illness, and drags you through the whole of its symptoms, progress, and treatment.

NOVEMBER 19

The Holy Week in Rome is supposed to offer great attractions to all visitors; but, saving for the sights of Easter Sunday, I would counsel those who go to Rome for its own interest, to avoid it at that time. The ceremonies, in general, are of the most tedious and wearisome kind; the heat and crowd at every one of them, painfully oppressive; the noise, hub-bub, and confusion, quite distracting.

NOVEMBER 20

"THE HOLLY TREE," CHRISTMAS STORIES (1855)

I might greatly move the reader by some account of the innumerable places I have not been to, the innu-merable people I have not called upon or received, the innumerable social evasions I have been guilty of, solely because I am by original constitution and character a bashful man.

NOVEMBER 21

THE OLD CURIOSITY SHOP (1841)

The place through which he made his way at lei-sure, was one of those receptacles for old and curious things which seem to crouch in odd corners of this town, and to hide their musty treasures from the public eye in jealousy and distrust. There were suits of mail standing like ghosts in armour, here and there; fantastic carvings brought from monkish cloisters; rusty weapons of various kinds; distorted figures in china, and wood, and iron, and ivory; tapestry, and strange furniture that might have been designed in dreams. The haggard aspect of the little old man was wonderfully suited to the place; he might have groped among old churches, and tombs, and deserted houses, and gathered all the spoils with his own hands. There was nothing in the whole collection but was in keeping with himself; nothing that looked older or more worn than he.

NOVEMBER 22

GREAT EXPECTATIONS (1861)

When we were all out in the raw air and were steadily moving towards our business [of tracking the escaped convicts], I treasonably whispered to Joe, "I hope, Joe, we shan't find them." And Joe whispered to me, "I'd give a shilling if they had cut and run, Pip."

NOVEMBER 23

MARTIN CHUZZLEWIT (1844)

"Their office is a smash" [said Poll]; "a swindle altogether. But what's a Life Assurance Office to a Life! And what a Life Young Bailey's was!"

NOVEMBER 24

THE OLD CURIOSITY SHOP (1841)

[T]hey came upon a straggling neighbourhood, where the mean houses parcelled off in rooms, and windows patched with rags and paper, told of the populous poverty that sheltered there. The shops sold goods that only poverty could buy, and sellers and buyers were pinched and griped alike. Here were poor streets where faded gentility essayed with scanty space and shipwrecked means to make its last feeble stand, but tax-gatherer and creditor came there as elsewhere, and the poverty that yet faintly struggled was hardly less squalid and manifest than that which had long ago submitted and given up the game.

NOVEMBER 25

For the night-wind has a dismal trick of wandering round and round a building of [this] sort, and moaning as it goes; and of trying, with its unseen hand, the windows and the doors; and seeking out some crevices by which to enter. And when it has got in: as one not finding what it seeks, whatever that may be, it wails and howls to issue forth again.

NOVEMBER 26

It is the custom on the stage, in all good murderous melodramas, to present the tragic and the comic scenes, in as regular alternation, as the layers of red and white in a side of streaky bacon. The hero sinks upon his straw bed, weighed down by fetters and misfortunes; in the next scene, his faithful but unconscious squire regales the audience with a comic song. We behold, with throbbing bosoms, the heroine in the grasp of a proud and ruthless baron: her virtue and her life alike in danger, drawing forth her dagger to preserve the one at the cost of the other; and just as our expectations are wrought up to the highest pitch, a whistle is heard, and we are straightway transported to the great hall of the castle: where a grey-headed seneschal sings a funny chorus.

NOVEMBER 27

Poor Traddles! In a tight sky-blue suit that made his arms and legs like German sausages, or roly-poly puddings, he was the merriest and most miserable of all the boys. He was always being caned . . . and was always going to write to his uncle about it, and never did. After laying his head on the desk for a little while, he would cheer up somehow, begin to laugh again, and draw skeletons all over his slate, before his eyes were dry.

NOVEMBER 28

"You have delivered the little parcel I gave you for your old [prison] landlord, Sam?" [said Mr. Pickwick.]

"I have, sir," replied Sam. "He bust out a cryin', sir, and said you wos wery gen'rous and thoughtful, and he only wished you could have him innokilated for a gallopin' consumption, for his old friend as had lived here so long, wos dead, and he'd noweres to look for another."

NOVEMBER 29

As BLOODY QUEEN MARY, this woman has become famous, and as BLOODY QUEEN MARY, she will ever be justly remembered with horror and detestation in Great Britain. Her memory has been held in such abhorrence that some writers have arisen in later years to take her part, and to show that she was, upon the whole, quite an amiable and cheerful sovereign! "By their fruits ye shall know them," said OUR SAVIOUR. The stake and the fire were the fruits of this reign, and you will judge this Queen by nothing else.

NOVEMBER 30

"I am Josiah Bounderby of Coketown. I know the bricks of this town, and I know the works of this town, and I know the chimneys of this town, and I know the smoke of this town, and I know the Hands of this town. . . . They're real. When a man tells me anything about imaginative qualities . . . I know what he means. He means turtle soup and venison, with a gold spoon, and that he wants to be set up with a coach and six."

DECEMBER

As the day closed in, I still rambled through the streets, feeling a companionship in the bright fires that cast their warm reflection on the windows as I passed, and losing all sense of my own loneliness in imagining the sociality and kind-fellowship that everywhere prevailed. At length I happened to stop before a Tavern, and, encountering a Bill of Fare in the window, it all at once brought it into my head to wonder what kind of people dined alone in Taverns upon Christmas Day.

Master Humphrey's Clock (1840–41)

DECEMBER 1

GREAT EXPECTATIONS (1861)

[When] I took my place by Magwitch's side, I felt that that was my place henceforth while he lived.

For now my repugnance to him had all melted away, and in the hunted wounded shackled creature who held my hand in his, I only saw a man who had meant to be my benefactor, and who had felt affectionately, gratefully, and generously, towards me with great constancy through a series of years. I only saw in him a much better man than I had been to Joe.

DECEMBER 2

BLEAK HOUSE (1853)

[Mr. Krook] was short, cadaverous, and withered; with his head sunk sideways between his shoulders, and the breath issuing in visible smoke from his mouth, as if he were on fire within. His throat, chin, and eyebrows were so frosted with white hairs, and so gnarled with veins and puckered skin, that he looked from his breast upward, like some old root in a fall of snow.

DECEMBER 3
A TALE OF TWO CITIES (1859)

So much was closing in about the women who sat knitting, knitting, that they their very selves were closing in around a structure yet unbuilt, where they were to sit knitting, knitting, counting dropping heads.

DECEMBER 4
LITTLE DORRIT (1857)

"Nobody" [said Dr. Haggage] "comes here to ask if a man's at home, and to say he'll stand on the door mat till he is. Nobody writes threatening letters about money to this place. It's freedom, sir, it's freedom! . . . Elsewhere, people are restless, worried, hurried about, anxious respecting one thing, anxious respecting another. Nothing of the kind here, sir. We have done all that—we know the worst of it; we have got to the bottom, we can't fall, and what have we found? Peace. That's the word for it. Peace."

DECEMBER 5
"A CHRISTMAS CAROL," CHRISTMAS BOOKS (1843)

"Are there no prisons?" asked Scrooge.
"Plenty of prisons," said the gentleman. . . .

"And the Union workhouses?" demanded Scrooge. "Are they still in operation?"

"They are. Still," returned the gentleman, "I wish I could say they were not."

"The Treadmill and the Poor Law are in full vigour, then?" said Scrooge.

"Both very busy, sir."

"Oh! I was afraid, from what you said at first, that something had occurred to stop them in their useful course," said Scrooge. "I'm very glad to hear it."

DECEMBER 6

THE OLD CURIOSITY SHOP (1841)

There are chords in the human heart—strange, varying strings—which are only struck by accident; which will remain mute and senseless to appeals the most passionate and earnest, and respond at last to the slightest casual touch.

DECEMBER 7

AMERICAN NOTES (1842)

It is the third morning. I am awakened out of my sleep by a dismal shriek from my wife, who demands to know whether there's any danger. I rouse myself, and look out of bed. The water-jug is plunging and leaping like a lively dolphin; all the smaller articles are afloat, except my shoes, which are stranded on a carpet-bag, high and dry, like a couple of coal-barges. Suddenly I see them spring into the air, and behold the looking-glass, which is nailed to the wall, sticking fast upon the ceiling. At the same time the door entirely disappears, and a new one is opened in the floor. Then I begin to comprehend that the state-room is standing on its head.

DECEMBER 8

OUR MUTUAL FRIEND (1865)
(A BALLAD BY SILAS WEGG)

Beside that cottage door, Mr. Boffin,
    A girl was on her knees;
She held aloft a snowy scarf, sir,
    Which (my eldest brother noticed) fluttered
        in the breeze.
She breathed a prayer for him, Mr. Boffin;
    A prayer he coold not hear.
And my eldest brother lean'd upon his sword,
    Mr. Boffin,
    And wiped away a tear.

DECEMBER 9

Of all my books, I like this the best. It will be easily believed that I am a fond parent to every child of my fancy, and that no one can ever love that family as dearly as I love them. But, like many fond parents, I have in my heart of hearts a favourite child. And his name is DAVID COPPERFIELD.

DECEMBER 10

Mr. Chadband is a large yellow man, with a fat smile, and a general appearance of having a good deal of train oil in his system. . . . Mr. Chadband moves softly and cumbrously, not unlike a bear who has been taught to walk upright . . . and never speaks without first putting up his great hand, as delivering a token to his hearers that he is going to edify them.

"My friends," says Mr. Chadband, "Peace be on this house! On the master thereof, on the mistress thereof, on the young maidens, and on the young men! My friends, why do I wish for peace? What is peace? Is it war? No. Is it strife? No. Is it lovely, and gentle, and beautiful, and pleasant, and serene, and joyful? O yes! Therefore, my friends, I wish for peace, upon you and upon yours."

DECEMBER 11

BARNABY RUDGE (1841)

At this same house, one of the [Gordon rioters] who went through the rooms, breaking the furniture and helping to destroy the building, found a child's doll—a poor toy—which he exhibited at the window to the mob below, as the image of some unholy saint which the late occupants had worshipped.

DECEMBER 12

AMERICAN NOTES (1842)

Schools may be erected, . . . pupils be taught, and masters reared . . . ; colleges may thrive, churches may be crammed, temperance may be diffused, and advancing knowledge in all other forms walk through the land with giant strides: but while the newspaper press of America is in, or near, its present abject state, high moral improvement in that country is hopeless. Year by year, it must and will go back; year by year, the tone of public feeling must sink lower down; year by year, the Congress and the Senate must become of less account before all decent men; and year by year, the memory of the Great Fathers of the Revolution must be outraged more and more, in the bad life of their degenerate child.

DECEMBER 13

BLEAK HOUSE (1853)

Fog everywhere. Fog up the river, where it flows among green aits and meadows; fog down the river, where it rolls defiled among the tiers of shipping, and the waterside pollutions of a great (and dirty) city. Fog on the Essex marshes, fog on the Kentish heights. Fog creeping into the cabooses of collier-brigs; fog lying out on the yards, and hovering in the rigging of great ships; fog drooping on the gunwales of barges and small boats. Fog in the eyes and throats of ancient Greenwich pensioners, wheezing by the firesides of their wards.

DECEMBER 14

"OUR HONOURABLE FRIEND,"
REPRINTED PIECES (1868)

Our honourable friend has sat in several parliaments, and given bushels of votes. He is a man of that profundity in the matter of vote-giving, that you never know what he means. When he seems to be voting pure white, he may be in reality voting jet black. When he says Yes, it is just as likely as not—or rather more so—that he means No.

DECEMBER 15

In every English-speaking home, in the four quarters of the globe, parents and children will do well to read Dickens aloud of a winter's evening; they will love winter, and one another, and God the better for it. What a wreath that will be of ever-fresh holly, thick with white berries, to hang to this poet's memory—the very crown he would have chosen.

DECEMBER 16

"DICKENS: THE MAN WHO INVENTED CHRISTMAS"
PHILIP ALLINGHAM ON THE VICTORIAN WEB
(DECEMBER 14, 2009)

One of his sons wrote that, for Dickens, Christmas was "a great time, a really jovial time, and my father was always at his best, a splendid host, bright and jolly as a boy and throwing his heart and soul into everything that was going on. . . . And then the dance! There was no stopping him!" Amateur magician and actor, Dickens had little Christmas shopping to worry about, and no crowded malls or crass commercialization of the family festival to jangle his finely-tuned nerves. But that time in his boyhood, when he slaved in the blacking factory while his family were in the Marshalsea Prison, weighed heavily somewhere in the back of his mind, and made occasional intrusions.

DECEMBER 17
MARTIN CHUZZLEWIT (1844)

You couldn't walk about in Todgers's neighbourhood, as you could in any other neighbourhood. You groped your way for an hour through lanes and bye-ways, and court-yards, and passages; and you never once emerged upon anything that might be reasonably called a street. A kind of resigned distraction came over the stranger as he trod those devious mazes, and, giving himself up for lost, went in and out and round about and quietly turned back again when he came to a dead wall or was stopped by an iron railing, and felt that the means of escape might possibly present themselves in their own good time, but that to anticipate them was hopeless. Instances were known of people who, being asked to dine at Todgers's, had travelled round and round for a weary time, with its very chimney-pots in view; and finding it, at last, impossible of attainment, had gone home again with a gentle melancholy on their spirits, tranquil and uncomplaining. Nobody had ever found Todgers's on a verbal direction, though given within a minute's walk of it. Cautious emigrants from Scotland or the North of England had been known to reach it safely, by impressing a charity-boy, town-bred, and bringing him along with them; or by clinging tenaciously to the postman; but these were rare exceptions, and only went to prove the rule that Todgers's was in a labyrinth, whereof the mystery was known but to a chosen few.

DECEMBER 18

LITTLE DORRIT (1857)

The rain fell heavily on the roof, and pattered on the ground, and dripped among the evergreens, and the leafless branches of the trees. The rain fell heavily, drearily. It was a night of tears.

If Clennam had not decided against falling in love with Pet; if he had had the weakness to do it; if he had, little by little, persuaded himself to set all the earnestness of his nature, all the might of his hope, and all the wealth of his matured character, on that cast; if he had done this and found that all was lost: he would have been, that night, unutterably miserable. As it was—

As it was, the rain fell heavily, drearily.

The child made a strong effort, but it was an unsuccessful one. . . . [He] wept until the tears sprung out from between his chin and bony fingers.

"Well!" exclaimed Mr. Bumble, stopping short, and darting at his little charge a look of intense malignity. "Well! Of *all* the ungratefullest and worst-disposed boys as ever I see, Oliver, you are the—"

"No, no, sir," sobbed Oliver, clinging to the hand which held the well-known cane; "no, no sir; I will be good indeed; indeed, indeed I will, sir! I am a very little boy, sir; and it is so—so—"

"So what?" inquired Mr. Bumble in amazement.

"So lonely, sir! So very lonely!" cried the child. "Everybody hates me. Oh! sir, don't, don't pray be cross to me!" The child beat his hand upon his heart; and looked in his companion's face, with tears of real agony.

Mr. Bumble regarded Oliver's piteous and helpless look with some astonishment, for a few seconds; hemmed three of four times in a husky manner; and, after muttering something about "that troublesome cough," bade Oliver dry his eyes and be a good boy. Then once more taking his hand, he walked on with him in silence.

DECEMBER 20

THE SPECTATOR (1870)

The greatest humourist whom England ever produced,—Shakespeare himself certainly not excepted.

DECEMBER 21

THE PICKWICK PAPERS (1837)

Christmas was close at hand, in all his bluff and hearty honesty; it was the season of hospitality, merriment, and open-heartedness; the old year was preparing, like an ancient philosopher, to call his friends around him, and amidst the sound of feasting and revelry to pass gently and calmly away. Gay and merry was the time, and gay and merry were . . . the numerous hearts that were gladdened by its coming.

And numerous indeed are the hearts to which Christmas brings a brief season of happiness and enjoyment. How many families, whose members have been dispersed and scattered far and wide, in the restless struggles of life, are then reunited, and meet once again in that happy state of companionship and mutual good-will, which is a source of such pure and unalloyed delight.

Marley was dead, to begin with. There is no doubt whatever about that. The register of his burial was signed by the clergyman, the clerk, the undertaker, and the chief mourner. Scrooge signed it. And Scrooge's name was good upon 'Change for anything he chose to put his hand to.

Old Marley was dead as a door-nail.

Ours was the marsh country, down by the river, within, as the river wound, twenty miles of the sea. My first most vivid and broad impression of the identity of things, seems to me to have been gained on a memorable raw afternoon towards evening. At such a time I found out for certain, that this bleak place overgrown with nettles was the churchyard; and that Philip Pirrip, late of this parish, and also Georgiana wife of the above, were dead and buried; and that Alexander, Bartholomew, Abraham, Tobias, and Roger, infant children of the aforesaid, were also dead and buried; and that the dark flat wilderness beyond the churchyard, intersected with dykes and mounds and gates, with scattered cattle feeding on it, was the marshes; and that the low leaden line beyond was the river; and that the distant savage lair from which the wind was rushing, was the sea; and that the small bundle of shivers growing afraid of it all and beginning to cry, was Pip.

DECEMBER 24

THE PICKWICK PAPERS (1837)

"This," said Mr. Pickwick, looking round him, "this is, indeed, comfort."

"Our invariable custom," replied Mr. Wardle. "Everybody sits down with us on Christmas Eve, as you see them now—servants and all; and here we wait, until the clock strikes twelve, to usher Christmas in, and beguile the time with forfeits and old stories."

DECEMBER 25

"A CHRISTMAS CAROL," CHRISTMAS BOOKS (1843)

Running to the window, he opened it, and put out his head. No fog, no mist; clear, bright, jovial, stirring, cold; cold, piping for the blood to dance to; Golden sunlight; Heavenly sky; sweet fresh air; merry bells. Oh, glorious! Glorious!

"What's to-day?" cried Scrooge, calling downward to a boy in Sunday clothes, who perhaps had loitered in to look about him.

"Eh?" returned the boy, with all his might of wonder.

"What's to-day, my fine fellow?" said Scrooge.

DECEMBER 26

"A CHRISTMAS CAROL," CHRISTMAS BOOKS (1843)

[Scrooge] had no further intercourse with Spirits, but lived upon the Total Abstinence Principle, ever afterwards; and it was always said of him, that he knew how to keep Christmas well, if any man alive possessed the knowledge. May that be truly said of us, and all of us! And so, as Tiny Tim observed, God bless Us, Every One!

DECEMBER 27

OUR MUTUAL FRIEND (1865)

So, she leaning on her husband's arm, they turned homeward by a rosy path which the gracious sun struck out for them in its setting. And oh, there are days in this life, worth life and worth death. And oh, what a bright old song it is, that oh, 'tis love, 'tis love, 'tis love, that makes the world go round!

DECEMBER 28

MARTIN CHUZZLEWIT (1844)

"Do I not know," [said Mr. Pecksniff,] "that in the silence and the solitude of night, a little voice will whisper in your ear, Mr. Chuzzlewit, 'This was not well. This was not well, sir!'"

DECEMBER 29

GREAT EXPECTATIONS (1861)

"So," said my convict, turning his eyes on Joe in a moody manner, and without the least glance at me; "so you're the blacksmith, are you? Then I'm sorry to say, I've eat your pie."

"God knows you're welcome to it—so far as it was ever mine," returned Joe, with a saving remembrance of Mrs. Joe. "We don't know what you have done, but we wouldn't have you starved to death for it, poor miserable fellow-creatur.—Would us, Pip?"

The something that I had noticed before, clicked in the man's throat again, and he turned his back.... No one seemed surprised to see him, or interested in seeing him, or glad to see him, or sorry to see him, or spoke a word, except that somebody in the boat growled as if to dogs, "Give way, you!"

DECEMBER 30

Let us leave our old friend in one of those moments of unmixed happiness, of which, if we seek them, there are ever some, to cheer our transitory existence here. There are dark shadows on the earth, but its lights are stronger in the contrast. Some men, like bats or owls, have better eyes for the darkness than for the light. We, who have no such optical powers, are better pleased to take our last parting look at the visionary companions of many solitary hours, when the brief sunshine of the world is blazing full upon them.

DECEMBER 31

"We'll devote the evening, brother," exclaimed Wegg, "to prosecute our friendly move. And arterwards, crushing a flowing wine-cup—which I allude to brewing rum and water—we'll pledge one another. For what says the Poet?

> And you needn't, Mr. Venus, be your black
>   bottle,
> For surely I'll be mine,
> And we'll take a glass with a slice of lemon in it
>   to which you're partial,
> For auld lang syne."

Appendix

Perhaps I should explain that I was not required to provide an appendix nor was I given any indication that one would be welcome. I do not complain of such treatment nor label it, but careful readers will note the all-too-familiar pattern. Anyhow, here is a first-rate appendix, suitable for one of those days when things are sour outside (or in) and you need a little sadistic humor to see you through. This is from *Nicholas Nickleby* (1839). Take it from there.

Dotheboys Hall,
Thursday Morning.
Sir,

My pa requests me to write to you, the doctors considering it doubtful whether he will ever recuvver the use of his legs which prevents his holding a pen.

We are in a state of mind beyond everything, and my pa is one mask of brooses both blue and green likewise two forms are steeped in his Goar. We were kimpelled to have him carried down into the kitchen where he now lays. You will judge from this that he has been brought very low.

When your nevew that you recommended for a teacher had done this to my pa and jumped upon his body with his feet and also langwedge which I will not pollewt my pen with describing, he assaulted my ma with dreadful violence, dashed her to the earth, and drove her back comb several inches into her head. A very little more and it must have entered her skull. We have a medical certifiket that if it had, the tortershell would have affected the brain.

Me and my brother were then the victims of his feury since which we have suffered very much which leads us to the arrowing belief that we have received some injury in our insides, especially as no marks of violence are visible externally. I am screaming out loud all the time I write and so is my brother which takes off my attention rather and I hope will excuse mistakes.

The monster having sasiated his thirst for blood ran away, taking with him a boy of desperate caracter that he had excited to rebellyon, and a garnet ring belonging to my ma, and not having been apprehended by the constables is supposed to have been took up by some stage-coach. My pa begs that if he comes to you the ring may be returned, and that you will let the thief and assassin go, as if we prosecuted him he would only be transported, and if he is let go he is sure to be hung before long which will save us trouble and be much more satisfactory. Hoping to hear from you when convenient

I remain
Yours and cetrer
FANNY SQUEERS

P.S. I pity his ignorance and despise him.

Index of Sources

All quotations from Dickens's novels are taken from *The Oxford Illustrated Dickens*, 21 vols. (New York: Oxford University Press, 1987).

March 16, March 31, April 12, April 22, May 10, May 23, June (general), June 1, June 3, June 27, July 8, July 23, July 28, August 13, August 31, September 19, October 10, November 21, November 24, December 6

Oliver Twist, January 13, January 20, January 25, January 28, January 29, February 1, February 23, April 9, April 24, May 11, May 30, June 8, June 28, August 1, August 5, August 15, August 23, August 29, September 1, October 4, October 18, November 26, December 19

Our Mutual Friend, January 15, January 21, February 2, February 21, February 26, April 2, April 25, April 27, May 4, June 5, June 16, July 1, September 28, October 21, November 3, December 8, December 27, December 31

Pickwick Papers, The, February 7, February 14, March 3, March 15, April 5, April 29, May 7, May 14, June 11, July 21, August (general), August 3, August 19, September 9, September 16, September 18, September 25, October 8, October 17, October 31, November 10, November 28, December 21, December 24, December 30

Pictures from Italy, May 1, May 19, September 13, November 19

Reprinted Pieces, October 20, November 18, December 14

Sketches by Boz, January 6, January 10, February 6, February 11, February 19, March 5, March 12, March 24, March 27, March 29, April 21, May (general), May 24, June 12, July 14, August 7, September 14, October 11, October 30, November 11

Tale of Two Cities, A, January 12, January 14, February 9, February 17, March 8, September 6, September 27, October 28, December 3

Uncommercial Traveller, The, February 8, May 21, July 5, July 20, August 28, September (general), September 4, September 10, September 29, October 13, October 19

Sources for Quotes about Dickens

January 24: Twain, Mark. "Mark Twain in Washington." San Francisco *Alta California*. February 5, 1868.

June 4: Wilson, Edmund. "Dickens: The Two Scrooges." In *The Wound and the Bow: Seven Studies in Literature*, 62–63. Cambridge, MA: Houghton Mifflin, 1941.

June 10: "Mr. Charles Dickens." *The Times* (London). Friday, June 10, 1870.

June 21: Eliot, T. S. "Wilkie Collins and Dickens." *The Times Literary Supplement*. August 4, 1927, 462.

June 25: Shaw, George Bernard. Preface to *Great Expectations*, by Charles Dickens, xvii. New York: The Modern Library, 2001.

July 31: Orwell, George. "Charles Dickens." In *A Collection of Essays*, 71. New York: Harcourt, 1946.

August 10: Orwell, George. In *An Age Like This, 1920–1940*, edited by Sonia Orwell and Ian Angus, 416–17. Boston: David R. Godine, 2000.

September 21: Greene, Graham. "The Young Dickens." In *The Lost Childhood and Other Essays*, 56–57. London: Eyre and Spottiswoode. 1951.

November 6: Ruskin, John. "The Roots of Honour," *Unto This Last*. In *Selections and Essays by John Ruskin*, edited by Frederick William Roe, 316. New York: Charles Scribner's Sons, 1948.

November 8: Dostoevsky, F. M. *The Complete Works*, Vol. 21, p. 69. Leningrad: 'Tzdater'stiove hauka [Science]. 1980.

December 15: Santayana, George. *Soliloquies in England and Later Soliloquies*, 72–73. London: Constable, 1922.

December 16: Allingham, Philip V. "Dickens: The Man Who Invented Christmas." The Victorian Web. Last modified December 14, 2009. http://www.victorianweb.org/authors/dickens/xmas/pva63.html.

December 20: "Charles Dickens." *Spectator*, xliii (1870), 716.